# The Second Chance Shop
# & Other Stories

## Bette Bono

ISBN: 9798988335382

Library of Congress Control Number: 2023949633

Cover Photo: Andrew Knopp

Author Photo: Tod Bryant

Cover Design by All Things that Matter Press

Published in 2023 by All Things that Matter Press

To Jack and Marian
who believed in and found a beautiful second chance
&
To Alex, Jessie, and Andrew
who believe in the magic of words (all the time)
laughter (sometimes at me)
and love

# Table of Contents


The Second Chance Shop ...................................................................1

Chili ...................................................................................................9

Tompkins Avenue, Brooklyn, 1902 ..................................................13

Swim Long Island Sound ...................................................................19

Birdman ...........................................................................................25

Reflections on My Behavior ..............................................................29

Wish You Were Here ........................................................................33

The Bracelet .....................................................................................39

At The Diner, 1942 ............................................................................51

Life of Crime ....................................................................................53

Big Brother .......................................................................................59

Housesitting .....................................................................................63

Fortune Teller ...................................................................................71

Billina ..............................................................................................79

At Lunch ...........................................................................................85

High Rollers ......................................................................................89

Mix-Up .............................................................................................93

Zinnias .............................................................................................99

Lifestyle ...........................................................................................103

Suitable Female Occupation, 1905 ...................................................109

Miggs ...............................................................................................115

Bertie Franklin Wynesco ..................................................................119

Crossing the Desert, 1958 ........................................................................123

Field Trip .................................................................................................129

Gathering Hay .........................................................................................133

Vamp.........................................................................................................137

Sidewalk Sale ..........................................................................................139

Dreams......................................................................................................145

Bus Ride....................................................................................................149

Moving Forward .....................................................................................153

Fame and Other Stuff .............................................................................157

Skinny Dip................................................................................................161

# The Second Chance Shop

"What came in today?" Cherry asked when she could finally catch her breath. She had been running late that morning, what with sleeping in an extra few minutes, and the River Bridge being raised to let a boat go by, and some kind of construction work on the two-lane rural road she used to get into town. And it was Monday.

On her way inside the shop, she had flipped the sign from *Closed* to *Open*, plopped her handbag at her desk in the back office, grabbed and donned her Second Chance Shop employee lanyard, and hurried out to the front of the store to confer with Camilla.

Camilla, who had probably already been at the shop for an hour, and who had volunteered at Second Chance for longer than anyone could ever remember, and who was pushing sixty, or seventy, or eighty depending on who you talked to, was already sorting clothes, her face wrinkled up in concentration.

"What came in?" Camilla repeated. "Well, three paper bags plus one plastic garbage bag were left by the back door last night. One cardboard carton with housewares was on the front steps when I got here. And Donna came by early to drop off a few items left over after her tag sale. Linus is going to do a pickup from the donation bins later this afternoon, and Gil says he's got boxes to unload from his truck."

"Anything interesting?" Cherry asked. She had been working as manager for more than a year but was still fascinated by what the town citizenry gave away to the Second Chance Shop which was, according to the sign posted in the window, open from 9 a.m. to 4 p.m., Monday through Saturday, closed on major holidays. The sign also informed those who entered that all profits were donated to the Friends of the Cedar Town Hospital.

Camilla held up her hands, the right one a little bent from arthritis, and ticked off a list. "I haven't checked the housewares yet, but we got some good clothes. A couple of really nice winter jackets for kids which no one will want to look at in this heat but will be snapped up when it's back-to-school shopping time. I'll hold off putting them in the juvenile clothing section until the fall. We got one prom dress, mauve, with matching shoes and a handbag. A stack of jeans, some with holes but that's okay since kids like them with holes. *New* ones are sold with holes. Two pairs of corduroy pants—ditto on those going away until fall—plus some sweatshirts, including a few for men and a few extra-large. And t-shirts."

"Of course," Cherry said.

"Of course," Camilla echoed. "*T-shirts are us.* In today's haul we got some from the Gap, some from Old Navy, some plain, and a half-dozen that are tie-dyed and must have been from somebody's retirement celebration because they're all printed with the message *Retirement = Party Time!*"

Cherry laughed. "We need to start the washables—"

"The first load of washables is already out of the dryer," Camilla said. "A second load is tumbling, and a third is rinsing or spinning in the washer. Gil's probably already finished the first batch of ironing."

Cherry brushed back a strand of curly brown hair and looked apologetic. "I think you should be in charge of this place, Cami."

Camilla giggled. She had a wonderful giggle. It was a little-old-lady giggle, but mischievous at the same time. "No need to fret, dear. Being a worrywart can be a good and helpful thing. If you didn't double-check everything, every single day, we'd still be floundering. Our customers used to have to wind their way through a labyrinth of unwashed, un-ironed, unorganized stuff not sorted by sizes or seasons or sexes or anything. And before you took charge, Second Chance rarely turned a profit and rarely found new homes for all the nice items people donate."

Cherry looked at her gratefully. In truth, she was proud of what she had accomplished at Second Chance even though it wasn't a job she had sought out. After her husband had died, she had been content—or so she thought—to live quietly, reading, gardening, doing a little of this, a little of that.

But then the president of the Friends of the Hospital had called. She knew him, although not well. He'd been an acquaintance of her husband, an insurance salesman who was active in the Rotary Club. The Hospital Friends needed her, he said. Old Lady Farrington had given them her house on Main Street when she moved to a retirement community, and they'd moved the thrift shop in last year, but the whole place was still an unorganized mess. They needed someone who could take charge.

"Cherry, I think you'd be just right for this," he'd said. "William told me you worked for one of the big department stores in the city before you two moved up here. There aren't a lot of folks around that have that kind of experience. You'll be perfect. You must know pretty much all there is to know about stores and, you know, shopping and clothing and that kind of thing."

That was all a long time ago, Cherry pointed out. She had worked in accounting. She had never been a manager, never worked in sales, never supervised employees, or even volunteers. When she and William moved to Cedar Town, she had handled the business side of his small law practice, but that, too, was in the past.

But, as she offered excuses, she realized they all sounded hollow, even to herself. She was only fifty. Her husband had been gone for three years. There was only so much "living quietly" she could do. And it was for the hospital, where William had spent his last days, and the doctors, the nurses, everyone there had been so very kind. She had accepted the job before the phone call ended.

Second Chance had become something to do, a reason to get up early, stay up late, spend time on the computer, time on the phone, clean, organize, meet, set policies, keep books, schedule and train volunteers, and, finally, to turn a very nice profit for the Hospital Friends.

The bell over the door jangled as a gangly teenaged girl with an eyebrow ring made her entrance. She was holding a tall cup already beaded with drops of condensation. A pink straw emerged from the plastic lid on top.

Camilla approached the girl, looped an employee lanyard over her head and eyed the drink with interest. "What's the Cedar Town Smoothie flavor today, Hannah-baby?"

Hannah took a long, noisy slurp. "Guava with a lavender spritz. Kerry made it special for me. She said it's awesome, and it is."

Camilla put on a skeptical expression. "A lavender spritz you say? I've got some lavender liquid soap at home. Never considered drinking it, though. Maybe one day you'll come in with a Coca Cola or an A&W. Then I'll know what you're talking about."

Hannah grinned. "You know I don't like those effervescent drinks, Granny Cam."

"You mean carbonated?"

"Yeah, that," Hannah said. "But, you know, effervescent means the same thing. I googled it. They both mean fizzy."

"If you googled it, then it must be so. But let's get busy Miss I-don't-like-fizzy. Today I'm going to need you to help me sort the teen clothes. I'm counting on you to tell me what's cool and what's not."

Cherry smiled to herself. Hannah had been sent to them from the high school's guidance counselor who had phoned in desperation six months earlier. "Cherry, can you help me out? Principal Dunbar's at his wit's end with this girl. Truancy, talking back to the teachers, a school-yard catfight. He was threatening to expel her, but I've talked him down, and I think I've got his agreement to a kind of negotiated settlement if she commits to, uh, 'volunteer community service.'"

"Let me guess where," Cherry had said with a rueful laugh.

"I think you'll guess in one. Which is a good thing. If I don't produce a job assignment, contact person, and phone number in the next ten minutes, the deal's off, and he'll just kick her out."

Cherry had felt some trepidation when Hannah first appeared. She didn't have children of her own and had no experience with teens. But, she soon realized, she needn't have worried. Camilla, who had raised five children and had a hand in the lives of dozens more, had, within a very short period of time, coddled, scolded, listened to, teased, complimented, sung to, and laughed with Hannah until the girl was now … part of the family, she'd have to say.

Sometimes she thought it was odd to think of "family" in that way. For years, it had always been William and her. Both only children. Both on their own by the time they were twenty. But now things were changing, were different, and when she thought about family, she thought about the people at the Second Chance Shop.

Cherry heard a noise from behind her and saw Gil walking in, both hands encumbered by hangers that held neatly ironed shirts, blouses, and slacks. She noticed immediately that he had donned one of the rainbow-tie-dyed and now freshly laundered *Party Time!* t-shirts. Their eyes met, and he gave her a grin.

Gil had joined the team a few months ago, shortly after Hannah arrived. He had shown up one morning, dressed rather formally, looking out of place, she thought at first, looking like a bit of a pompous ass. He was medium height, with neat gray hair, blue eyes, and a long straight nose—what people used to call a patrician nose. He didn't look like the kind of person who shopped at a thrift store, but there he was.

She had approached him, asked if there was anything she could help him with, and explained that menswear was in the side parlor. He hadn't responded, but let his eyes roam around the shop, surveying the racks of clothing and the items on the display shelves. Finally he had studied her. Then he spoke.

"The womenfolk—well, my daughters—say I need to do something. To volunteer at something. I think they just want me out of the house."

"And what does your wife say?" she had said automatically, then realized, to her horror, the mistake she had made. She saw it immediately in the expression on his face, the same expression she had seen in the mirror at home after her husband had died. Many of the shop's volunteers were there because the hospital had cared for their loved ones, helped the families as the end drew near.

"I'm so sorry," she said. "I'm so sorry. Can we begin again?"

He gave the slightest nod, so she went on.

"We're always happy to have volunteers. And grateful. Is there a particular job you were interested in doing? Our accounting books are pretty basic. Maybe sales? Many of our customers are women, but we get men, too, and we also have a room with used sports equipment ...."

It was Camilla who had once again come to the rescue, albeit inadvertently, by arriving from the laundry room with a basket of shirts in need of pressing.

Gil had looked at the old woman holding the basket, then turned to Cherry. "I can iron," he said. "And I know how to polish shoes. I learned in the army a long time ago, before the uniforms were permanent press. This past year, I did all the laundry. When Val couldn't."

Cherry and Camilla had looked at each other. "Give the man an iron," Camilla had said, and they had, and now he, too, was part of the family.

As Gil arrived at work every day—and the days became weeks, then months—Cherry had learned he was not pompous at all. He was someone who was reserved in his grief. She understood because she, too, had grieved in that way. Many of the shop's volunteers and customers had, by word and example, taught her about grief and the many different forms it could take. For some it was a time of talk, for some a time of silence. For some it was busyness, for others lassitude. Some cried at a song on the radio, a photo, a memory. Some were stoic in the presence of others.

There had only been one time when she had seen Gil cry. It had been early on. He had suggested using one of the smaller rooms for donated books, and she had agreed. He had found bookshelves and moved some comfy armchairs into the room because, he explained, "Sometimes people need to sit with a book, get to know it for a while before they take it home."

One afternoon she had found him seated in one of those comfy chairs. He had told her the room was almost ready to be opened to the public. She had poured a glass of iced tea to bring him because it was a hot day, and he'd been carrying in boxes of books and arranging them on the shelves. As she walked in with the tea, she had been brought up short by the sight of Gil, seated, with a book open on his lap, tears streaming down his face.

When he saw her, he started and gathered himself as if collecting the energy needed to say something or explain, but she shook her head. There's no need, my friend, she thought, and it was as if he heard that thought because relief came over his features. Very quietly, she had placed the tea next to him, put a hand on his shoulder, then left him alone.

Slowly, gradually, as weeks and months went by, he began to be someone who could smile and tell jokes and play around. Someone who—she had, at some point, realized—encouraged her to do the same. Someone who worked hard, and did laundry, and ironed, and polished shoes, and fixed things that needed fixing, and charmed everyone who walked in the door.

Gil hung the ironed clothes on the rack labeled "New Arrivals" then spread his arms wide to model the *Party Time!* shirt.

"So nice of you to promote the new merchandise," Cherry said dryly.

"I knew as soon as I saw these shirts, I had to have one," he said. "It suits me, don't you think?" This last he addressed to Hannah.

The teen giggled. "I liked the *Star Wars* shirt you found last week, but that one's good, too." She took another long pull at the pink straw. "Speaking of 'party time,' I heard there was a skinny-dip party at River's Bend last weekend. They were talking about it at the smoothie shop. Kerry said it wasn't kids having the party. Just a couple older folks. Like *really* older. Like you guys. Anybody here know anything about that?"

"Don't be ridiculous, Hannah-baby," Camilla said dismissively. "I know River Bend's the best spot for cooling off and canoodling. Always has been, even in my day, and always will be. But with the mosquito population in August, any water-frolicking at dusk would mean mosquito-bite-scratching at dawn."

Hannah grinned.

Gil grinned, too, then oh so casually began to scratch his arm.

"Cherry," he asked innocently, "what did you say was the best way to stop the itch? Baking soda? I tried aloe vera, but it didn't seem to help much."

Camilla turned on him with a stern look. "*Gilbert James Brown*, there's a whole basket of laundry needing to be ironed, so take yourself off and iron it. *Now*."

Gilbert's grin grew a little wider, but he turned and sauntered from the room, still scratching. Cherry, Camilla, and Hannah looked at each other then burst into laughter. Cherry knew she was blushing, but somehow didn't care a bit.

They were still laughing when the bell over the door jangled again. The first customer had arrived. It was Monday, a sunny Monday, and another day at the Second Chance Shop had begun.

# Chili

The teenaged boy and the old man sat on the bleachers in the gym and surveyed the scene. Tables had been put up and covered with checked cloths. The three finalists stood at stations featuring large crockpots, Styrofoam bowls, plastic spoons, and paper napkins. A banner against one wall—prepared by Ms. Daniel's art students—announced the reason for the crowd of people gathered around the tables: *Benjamin Cardozo High School Annual Chili Cook-Off!*

The old man had parked his custodian's cleaning cart off to the side. The kid had opened a laptop and was typing away. He stopped, reread what he had written, then grimaced.

"I'm not sure I've got the description exactly right. This is my first big article for the school paper, and I want to get it right. I was comparing it to those TV cooking competition shows, but it's not really that. My mom likes those Food Network shows, you know, like *Chopped* and *Beat Bobby Flay.*"

"How about *Barbecue Battle*?" the old man asked. "Do you ever watch that one?"

The kid wrinkled his nose. "I've seen it a couple times. My mom thinks that one's a little high on the testosterone."

"I agree with your mom," the old man said with a grin.

"Yeah, she says the judges think they're on *Gunsmoke*," the kid said. "That's, like, an old TV show about cowboys."

"I think I've heard of it," the old man said.

"I don't think cooking should be all about, you know, competition, especially when it gets sorta like confrontation," the kid said. "It kinda takes the fun out of it. So, which of the finalists do you think is going to win?"

"You're asking my opinion? The janitor's opinion?"

"Of course I am. You know everything there is to know about what goes on here. You know each of those kids, probably better than anyone, and I saw you try each of the chilis, and you've worked here a bazillion years, and this isn't the first chili competition you've been to. And I know you're pals with Ms. Peterson who teaches Home Ec, so you've probably compared notes on the kids and cooking and stuff. And people who've lived a long time have tasted lots of chili, so you probably know what's good and what's only okay."

The old man grinned. "You're pretty perceptive for a kid reporter who's writing his first big article."

"Thank you. But really, I need your opinion. I could kinda work it into the article. I wouldn't quote you or anything because I know you wouldn't want to be seen as having favorites. But I could write something like 'some people felt that …,' or 'there was a sense that ….' You know, I'd keep it vague and anonymous. You could be like a confidential source. When we had a unit on journalism in English class, we talked about how you always have to protect your confidential sources."

"Okay, okay," the old man said with a laugh. "I suppose I can talk to you if it's all off the record. Now let me see. Laura's chili was delicious if you want a vegetarian version. Lots of vegetables, heavy on the beans, maybe, but the tomatoes and peppers are from her granny's garden, and no one grows better tomatoes or finer peppers than Mrs. Cooper."

"What about Frank's version?"

"Well, I have to say I liked the butternut squash and quinoa combination. I don't know if I'd call it chili, exactly, but it was pretty good."

"I saw you get seconds on that one."

"Yep."

"Frank told me he developed his recipe because beans always make him fart, but he likes all the other stuff in chili, the spices and stuff, so that's why he made it that way. He said it was twenty-first-century chili. You know, modern."

"Are you going to put that comment about farts in your article?"

The kid laughed. "I'd like to—I mean I'd really like to—but we'll see. Sometimes people don't like to read about, you know, reality and stuff. And I'm not sure discussing farting in an article about food sets the right tone. Okay, what about Tanya's chili?"

"I think that one's the winner."

The kid looked up from his laptop. "So you do have a favorite?"

"Don't get me wrong, I liked all the chilis, and I like all the kids, and this is a good event. But what Tanya did was a good classic chili, and when she served it out, she asked everyone if they wanted more beans or more meat or more vegetables, and told them she made it just medium hot, so no one was going to get overcome with the heat-level and get embarrassed by coughing out food in front of their friends. Which isn't cool when you're in high school."

"So, the winner is the friendliest chili?"

"Yep, I guess that's it. Sure, you gotta have a good recipe, but part of cooking is the presentation, too, and the feeling you get when someone's serving you something they made."

"The friendliest chili," the kid repeated. He typed the words, then typed a bit more, then looked at the screen admiringly. "I think this is going to be a fun article," he said. "It's not really about winning, is it? It's about the process. It's about the people."

"I think you're onto something there," the old man said. "You're onto a pretty good recipe."

# Tompkins Avenue, Brooklyn, 1902

Miriam had been present when the Michtoms first discussed the idea of offering little stuffed animal dolls in their candy shop on Tompkins Avenue in Brooklyn. Her papa and Mr. Michtom were friends, having both arrived from Russia as teenagers on the same boat.

When Mama died shortly after giving birth to Ruth, Mrs. Michtom—Rose—had taken Miriam under her wing. The Michtoms had even offered her employment that was better and safer and so much happier than sewing by hand or on a pedal machine in one of the crowded sweatshops on the East Side where whole families spent their days making lace, sewing buttons on shirtwaists, or fashioning gloves.

"Send Miriam and Ruth to us during the day," Mr. Michtom had told Papa. "Miriam can watch Ruth and our little Emily and help out in the shop."

Tears had come to Papa's eyes, and the two men had shaken hands. Papa had turned to her, and she saw, beyond the tears, the relief he felt.

"Mr. Michtom is the kindest man I know," he told her.

Now, Miriam arrived promptly every morning before the shop opened, holding her little sister by the hand. Her days were full, but somehow fascinating, wonderful, so different from the experiences of most of her friends. In addition to caring for the two little girls, she lent a hand in the shop. In the morning she set out the bins of candy, the Tootsie Rolls wrapped in little squares of paper and the heart-shaped, sugary Sweethearts. She could attend to customers when the shop was busy and help with the cleaning and close-up at the end of the day.

She thought often of Papa's words and found them to be true. Mr. Michtom never seemed cross or impatient. When the workday was over, he would insist that she choose a piece of candy for herself.

What was a revelation to Miriam was the banter between the Michtoms, the way they talked and talked and *talked*. About the shop, the customers, the neighborhood, the old country, the past, the future, the news, their family, their daughter, their friends, everything.

It was Rose who had first suggested they start sewing stuffed toy animals to attract more children to the shop window.

"You are a clever shopkeeper, are you not, Mr. Michtom?" Rose began.

"I hope so, my dear," he replied. Miriam could tell he knew his wife had something in mind.

"If a child peers in the window and sees something wonderful, an animal doll with a friendly face, with luck he will head toward the door, pulling his mother or father by the hand."

"That is so," her husband agreed.

"The children will have pennies for the candy," Rose went on. "Mother and Father will have more than pennies for the stuffed toy. We have both plied a needle. I can fashion the patterns. We can make the animals that are at the Zoological Garden at Prospect Park. Deer and sheep and a seal."

"Shall we create Michtom's Menagerie, then?" Morris looked at his wife with amusement. "Shall I become the next P.T. Barnum?"

"There will be grandparents remembering Barnum's American Museum and the animals on display there," Rose said. "Grandparents with more than pennies who could be coaxed into purchasing a Jumbo the Elephant doll."

Rose's plan had worked. Both of the Michtoms could, indeed, ply a needle. Miriam could as well. It was a skill many an immigrant used to make a living in the New World. Often the first place a new arrival went to after Ellis Island, was the square in lower Manhattan where contractors collected employees who could sew.

Miriam had also helped create the paper patterns for the animals, cut the pieces from the plush fabrics, stitch and stuff the toys, add button eyes, and embroider noses, whiskers, and paws.

The idea for a stuffed bear had come from Mr. Michtom. He had brought home a newspaper obtained from one of the newsies that sold them on the street corners. The new president, Theodore Roosevelt, who had come to office the previous year after the shocking assassination of President McKinley, had been on a hunting trip in Mississippi with Governor Longino. Roosevelt had refused to shoot a bear that had been tied to a tree for him for that purpose. He didn't feel it was sporting or fair, and the incident had been publicized in a cartoon. Mr. Michtom showed the cartoon to Rose and Miriam.

"Can you make a bear?" he asked. "This bear? The president's bear?"

Rose studied the cartoon then handed it to Miriam. "Velvet plush, don't you think, my dear?"

"Yes," Miriam agreed. "With a lighter color for the paws. Those little black buttons for the eyes. And round ears. We can make it a cub, like in the drawing. Children will want to hold it and care for it." She eyed Ruth and Emily sitting on the carpet, playing together in the sun. "Everyone will see that even the president has a soft spot for a little bear."

It hadn't taken long. When Miriam arrived the next morning, the cub was sitting in the window, surrounded by candy. Mr. Michtom had saved the cartoon from the newspaper, and it was placed by the toy for all to see, along with a little sign: *Teddy's Bear.*

"I made five bears last night," Rose said when Miriam entered the shop. "I was up so late into the night, but I told Morris we needed to have them ready. The bear in the window will bring in the customers. The other bears will go home with the customers."

Somehow, Miriam knew Rose would be proven right, and she was. By the end of the day, the only bear left was the one in the window. Rose had declared that one was not to be sold.

Miriam was not surprised to hear Rose begin another colloquy as they pulled the shades at the end of the day and began the cleaning and set up for the next day's business.

"We will need more bears, Mr. Michtom," she pointed out. "We sold one of the elephants and a sheep, but it is the bears the children want, Teddy's bear."

"I believe you are right, my dear," Mr. Michtom replied. He thought a minute. "I believe it is the popularity of the president that makes the bears desirable. People still remember the two years Mr. Roosevelt spent as police commissioner. The papers were full of news of his work, the way he battled corruption.

Rose nodded. "He insisted that a policeman should be more than a thug. He made a difference that has lasted. And it has only been five years since he left the city to go on to even greater things. Do you think, Mr. Michtom, that we ought to write to the president? We could tell him of the popularity of the bear and ask his permission to name these animal dolls Teddy bears."

Mr. Michtom had been filling one of the large glass jars with wrapped Hub Wafers, but he paused and looked at his wife. "That would be the right thing to do," he said, "and a fine thing to do. And we will send him a bear so he may see the animal doll that, with his permission, will bear his name."

The month that followed was one of the most exciting of Miriam's life. She had not thought it could be so, but it was. The bears continued to sell. The shop had never been busier, and the Michtoms had started tucking a few extra bills into Miriam's hand as the girl stayed up late crafting more bears along with her employers. The crowning moment had come just last week when a letter had arrived from the White House.

Mr. Michtom had gathered his family and insisted Miriam's Papa be present as well. With trembling hands he had opened the envelope, read the message, then passed it to his wife.

"He has granted his permission," Rose said. "I can scarce believe it. I don't know what to say."

At this, Mr. Michtom laughed. "I believe that condition will be temporary."

Rose had laughed, too, and handed the note to Papa.

"Listen," Papa had said. "He writes 'I don't think my name is likely to be worth much in the bear business, but you're welcome to use it.' What a kind and gracious thing. His name will be worth very much. A name is important if it is a good name from a good man."

Papa reached out to hand the note back to Rose, but she demurred. "Show Miriam," she said.

Miriam took the note and read the words, marveling that the paper she held had been held by the president of the United States.

Mr. Michtom sighed with happiness. "How many bears will we need for next week? I believe once this note is on display with the bear in the window, every child in New York City will want a Teddy bear."

"It is not just the children who want the bears," Miriam said, then flushed.

"Tell me," Mr. Michtom said.

Miriam glanced at Rose who nodded her head. The older woman knew what had sparked the comment.

Miriam looked at her papa, then back at Mr. Michtom. "Today a man came in with his wife. I thought they had come for the sweets, but he selected a bear, one I had made with a pink nose. He purchased it, then put it into his wife's arms, and she hugged it and gave the smallest of smiles. Do you think they may be expecting a child?"

"Perhaps," Rose answered, "or hoping for one. Or perhaps they have lost one. There are many times when it may be good to hug a small bear."

Miriam thought of the night Ruth had been born and the night, not so many months later, that had taken her mother away forever.

Mr. Michtom had listened to Miriam and his wife and now seemed thoughtful. Finally, he smiled and went over to the display of stuffed animals. They were now as prominently featured as the jars filled with candies. He seemed to study each of the animal dolls carefully, then selected a pretty one, one that Miriam had made. It had been fashioned with beautiful brown fur, and she had tied a bright red bow around its neck.

Turning to Miriam, he placed the bear in her arms. "Today is a special day," he said, "a happy day. You have earned something more today than an extra piece of candy. Thank you for all you have done, and thank you for teaching me something tonight."

Miriam took the bear and folded her arms around it. "But I haven't …."

"You have, my child. You and Mrs. Michtom have taught me that there are many times—and many people—that can be made to feel better by hugging a small bear."

# Swim Long Island Sound

They sat on a bench set back from the crowded beach. Callie thought about how they must look to others. An elderly couple, carefully dressed, he in long pants, a lightweight blazer, a rather jazzy cap. She in a summer dress with a sweater thrown over her shoulders. They looked, she thought, the way someone should look on the veranda of a shoreline restaurant. Ready for a waiter to offer them a drink. A gin and tonic, perhaps.

They certainly didn't look like a couple that would run off into the surf, sit on a blanket on the sand, or slather lotion on each other's backs. They looked too old for that. No one looking at them would think that. Callie giggled. Little did they know.

Rick put his arm around her. "What are you thinking about?"

"I'm thinking no one knows what we're up to. What we've been up to for the last six months."

"You mean no one knows we're the coaching team for Mr. Eugene Barry, the oldest swimmer that's qualified for the Swim Long Island Sound open-sea marathon? The coaching team that's fudged the rules, lied on his application, and successfully misled the organizers of that fine charity event as to who, exactly, that solo contestant is? How old that contestant is?"

"We didn't really fudge the rules, at least not any important ones," Callie said with a touch of asperity. "And we already decided that what we did was worth it, and important, from a fighting ageism standpoint. So let's do what we came to do and go over everything again."

"Yes, ma'am," he said. "Where do we start?"

"Now this is where the swimmers head out, right?"

They took a moment and scanned the long shoreline. The sand was filled with blankets and beach chairs, parents were rubbing lotion on the backs of children, teens were wading into the water, splashing each other, laughing.

"Yes, when the beach closes tonight, they'll set up everything they need for the race. The escort boats will be at the marina, and staff will be along the pier. They're doing the awards ceremony and the party at the pavilion on the Connecticut side."

"Tomorrow, what time do the swimmers take off?"

He looked at his watch as if to remind himself of the information. "They'll go out in three waves. The first will leave at 8:15, the second at 9:00, the last at 9:45. Eugene lucked out and got himself in the first wave."

"And what time do they expect the contestants to start coming in?"

"Well, the lead swimmers should be arriving …," he calculated a moment in his head, "about 3:00 or so."

"So, seven hours in the water?"

"Yes. Some will take much longer, of course—like our man—but there's a time limit. If you haven't come in after nine-and-a-half hours, they'll have an escort boat pull you out."

"And as soon as the last swimmer comes in, there's the awards ceremony, and the post-swim marathon party."

"I imagine the party is more for the non-swimmers, you know, the sponsors, medical staff, and corporate donors. I think the swimmers will want to crawl under the covers and sleep for about ten or twelve hours."

Callie grinned. "Somehow, I don't think Eugene will. The way he talks, he says he's going to dance the night away."

Rick grinned, too, then pulled his face into a more serious expression. "Let's go over the rules again. Just so we're clear on what we've done and not done. Which *I*'s we've not dotted and *T*'s we've not crossed."

Callie nodded. "Well, like I said, we've pretty much followed the rules. Pretty much. Everybody at the senior center pitched in what they could, so we submitted the five-hundred-dollar entry fee, cash on the barrel."

"Nobody requires cash on the barrel anymore," he noted. "I'm sure they happily took PayPal or a credit card or some other new-fangled money-transfer app from the other applicants."

"Well, we turned in cash. I thought it was touching the way folks put in their five- and ten-dollar bills. They wanted those bills turned in. *I* wanted those bills turned in. The ones they had taken out of their wallets. Everyone wanted to see one of us, a senior, compete. Now what else?"

"You gotta wear a regulation suit. A man's suit can't cover his torso. No suit can go below the knees. Suits can't cover the shoulders in any way. No wetsuits, of course. If you want to, you can wear a cap, goggles, earplugs, and grease. But no flotation aids, propulsion devices, fins, hand paddles, pull buoys, or boards."

"What's the grease for? Remind me."

"Some think it helps prevent chafing. Some say it helps insulate the body in cold water. Some say it doesn't do squat, but there's a placebo effect." He shrugged. "Eugene says he's not using it."

"Eugene says he won't need it, because …," Callie started giggling again, "because he's the product of an affair between a mermaid and a lighthouse keeper and the open water is his second home."

"That's what he says when he's had more than one-too-many," Rick said.

"Yep. He also says that if he had his druthers, he'd do the swim naked—no grease, no suit—but he knows he's got to wear regulation swimwear, so that's what he'll do. Now let's talk about the qualifying swim. That's the one requirement that was a stumbling block. Obviously, the swim organizers don't want a bunch of hotdoggers diving in the water to show off for the cameras and the girls, then pooping out big-time in the middle of the sound. So, to enter as a solo swimmer, you have to do a qualifying six-hour open sea swim—"

"Or," Rick interrupted, "show proof that you've completed a league-approved swim—like across the English Channel or that Jersey Shore swim—"

"Within the previous eighteen months." Callie finished the sentence.

"Yes."

They looked at each other.

"Eugene showed us what he can do," Callie said. "When he swam back and forth at the park district municipal pool—all night long. All night long! Ten p.m. to six a.m. in that big, outdoor, Olympic pool."

"After we bribed Mr. Radcliffe to let us stay past closing time," Rick added, "and paid that nice lifeguard kid to pull an all-nighter on site.

The kid wasn't needed. We weren't needed. I almost started believing Eugene's story about his mermaid mother. I don't think it was too wrong of us to forge that 'open-sea' swim certificate."

"A pool, even an outdoor pool, is not open water. It's a different swimming experience," Callie pointed out.

"True, and I keep turning that over in my head. But remember," he paused and took her hand, "remember that time we went to Calf Pasture Beach in Norwalk? Remember what he did?"

Callie shuddered. "Of course I remember. I thought he was dead for sure."

"We all thought he was dead," Rick said. "After the weather turned that afternoon, it came time to get back in the van to go back to the residences, and no one could find him. Then someone said he had gone for a swim, but that was hours earlier. And we were just about to call 911 when he comes waltzing up, dripping wet in his suit and says he thought the Norwalk Islands looked so 'cute' from the shore that he decided to head over and check them out. And he was having so much 'fun' he decided to swim over and do a loop around the Sheffield Island Lighthouse for good measure.

"And you've seen him when we go to the beach. Even when he stays near the shore, he's not just an observer. He's like them." Rick waved his hand toward the swimmers in the water, the children wading in the surf, the teens standing on each other's shoulders and diving in, the adults swimming a bit farther out, paralleling the shore.

"You're right," Callie agreed. "He's a participant. He's not one to sit on the sidelines. Not if he's near the water." She watched the activity for a moment before saying anything else. "Why are we so sure Eugene can do this? He's old, like us."

"You know that lady who went to UConn? Elizabeth Fry? She did a two-way swim across the English Channel when she was fifty-two."

"Eugene is sixty-two, at least. And it's not as if he's going to win."

"He doesn't care about winning. He doesn't care if he comes in last. He doesn't care about setting a record as the oldest veteran to complete the swim, or oldest Connecticut resident, or oldest anything at all. He just wants to do it for himself. He wants to participate. Young people do that all the time. They do things for themselves. He wants to know he can set himself a goal and accomplish it. Just that."

"Not a bad desire."

"Not bad at all."

Rick leaned over and kissed her cheek. "Want to go in the water?"

"I'm not dressed for it."

"Me neither, but they've got changing rooms by the pier. I grabbed our suits and stuck them in a tote bag. Just in case. I'm game if you are."

She smiled. "Of course I'm game. I'm always game. Let's do it. Then let's get back and make sure our boy goes to bed early. Tomorrow's going to be a very big day."

# Birdman

No one knows how Birdman got his name. He just kinda introduced himself that way when he joined up with us. He was just another kid on a bike—a bike put together with old parts like the ones we all rode. A kid with a baseball glove. He showed up at the empty lot one day, riding up, stopping but not dismounting. He knew the etiquette of the matter, stayed, and watched, and waited for one of us to ask if he wanted to play.

One idea we had about his name was that he called himself that because of the movie, *The Birdman of Alcatraz*. Who wouldn't wanna be Burt Lancaster? Especially if you're ten or eleven or twelve, and it's 1962, and you're in Chicago—one of the tough parts of Chicago—and you don't have much, and even with a bike, no matter where you go, you're sorta locked in, so it feels kinda like a penitentiary. At least a penitentiary from a kid's understanding.

Plus, when a bunch of the grandpas got together on the stoops, they'd talk about the *calaboose,* and you've known kids, some older kids, who'd been rounded up by the cops. Back then, the Cook County Jail had its own electric chair. And Stateville was pretty close by. Joliet, too.

You shoulda seen the lines outside the Palace Theater the summer that Burt Lancaster picture came out. We all saw it together at the late show. It had to be the late show because that's when Louie's brother, who was an usher, was working and could let us in by opening the side door right down by the screen. We woulda liked a matinee better because that's when all the kids would be there, and you'd see everybody and be seen yourself. And there'd be something dramatic about going from the light and heat of the sidewalks into a theater that wasn't just named a palace, it was a palace. Maybe you'd have some popcorn and get a good seat with all your friends, and then the lights would go down, and you'd be somewhere magical for a while.

For myself, I don't think Birdman took his name from Burt Lancaster. It was more likely just who he was. Like if you watched him play ball, you'd see the bird inside the kid. On that first game, when we asked him if he wanted to play, we put him in the outfield, 'cause if you don't know how a kid will do, you start him in the outfield. We saw he was going to be fine when a long fly ball was sent his way, a fly ball that—if everything we knew about fly balls and the universe held true—shoulda cleared the fence and boomeranged down the alley behind the grocer's and Levine's Tailors and Dry Cleaners. But somehow Birdman was in the air, too many feet above the ground to be real, with his arm up and his glove ready, and the ball just slapped into that glove like a magnet pulled it there.

Birdman could throw, too. Like Willie Mays could throw. Like a magician that makes a dove appear outa nowhere, he could throw a ball into the sky, and it'd soar like a bird and land just where it should, safely in someone else's glove.

Birdman was only with us for about a year, but we liked him real fine, and he made a difference in an interesting kinda way, just from some of the things he did. Like saving Mr. Levine's cat. That's the thing that got to me. In the kiddy books they'd give you in elementary school to learn how to read, there'd sometimes be a story about a cat getting stuck up in a tree. The pictures in the book would show a fireman coming to the rescue in his truck and going up a ladder to bring the cat down and putting it in the arms of a pretty little girl in a pink dress.

Well, first off, there weren't any trees in our part of Chicago, not back then, anyway, and the fire department wasn't likely to show up to help when a bad-tempered feline that only liked Mr. Levine and no one else got herself stuck up on a fire escape and didn't know what to do next.

We'd been riding by on our bikes and stopped to see what was what because it was unusual to see old Mr. Levine out of his shop. He was pointing up at the cat and going back and forth in English and, I don't know, his other kinda language that maybe was German, and he was sorta crying and trying to explain to a couple folks there on the sidewalk that the cat wouldn't come down.

We might've just kept going, but Birdman got off his bike and went up to Mr. Levine, and stood there with his head to the side, like he was considering what he might be able to do. Then he put his hand on Mr. Levine's arm, right where the numbers were tattooed, and said, "Can I help?"

Mr. Levine looked at Birdman and a tear rolled down his cheek, and he said, "Robin, she go out the window. She won't come down."

Birdman says, "Your cat's name is Robin?"

Mr. Levine says, "Yes, yes, Robin," and Birdman grins, and pats the old man's arm, and goes right over to that old fire escape and stands underneath it and looks up.

I don't know if you know what those fire escapes are like on those old brick buildings, but they're designed a lot more for going down than going up. Like there's platforms on every story of the building and ladders to go down, but the ladder on the lowest level doesn't go down to the ground but is held up by a hinge. If you're going down you can undo the hinge and lower the ladder, but you can't reach that level from the street.

But Birdman, after he spends a minute looking up at all those metal bars and railings and ladders, it's just like he's on the baseball field. He jumps into the air higher than you think anyone could and gets hold of a bar on the bottom platform. You could see his stomach below the edge of his t-shirt as he was hanging there, and you could see there was a hole in one of his gym shoes, but he only hangs there a minute before he pulls himself up and starts to climb.

All of us down on the sidewalk were watching him. There was our gang and Mr. Levine, and a couple men from some of the other shops, and some of the people who had just been walking by and stopped to see what was happening. In that moment, Birdman showed all of us, showed everyone, that you could rise, and climb, and scramble, and be a hero, even if you didn't have a lot else going for you. Even if you were only a kid.

So, yeah, he got up to the cat, who maybe recognized him as a fellow creature that had some kinship with her on account of their names, and somehow decided Birdman didn't deserve to be scratched to pieces. We see Birdman pick her up and tuck her under his t-shirt, right against his chest, so she's kinda cradled like a little baby. Then he stands up and works his way down.

When Birdman is back on earth, he takes Robin out from under his t-shirt and places her in Mr. Levine's arms. The old man hugs her to his own chest and pulls the sides of his sweater around her. Then he pulls

Birdman close and hugs him and cries a little more and says stuff to Birdman that's probably thank you.

The crying and hugs, for pretty much anyone else, would have been … I don't know … not done or embarrassing or something. But Birdman just hugged him back like he understood the etiquette of that moment, like he'd understood the etiquette of the sandlot when we first met him.

At the end, he smiled at Mr. Levine, rubbed the cat on her ears, then picked up his bike and got on, and it was the signal for the rest of us to head on down the street.

One day Birdman tells us he's moving away. His folks got an apartment on the south side, closer to the steel mill where his old man worked. Then he wasn't there, and we found somebody else for the outfield. But Birdman stayed in our heads in a certain way, at least in my head. Sometimes you learn stuff from someone, even if you're not really paying attention. Birdman showed that you could soar, like Willie Mays, like a magician, like Burt Lancaster. And even if you had a kinda prison around you, you could climb, and fly, and be free, and be a birdman.

# Reflections on My Behavior

Okay, so I'm supposed to write this essay because I was caught smoking in the bathroom with Lacey Sanderson, and I guess things could've turned out a whole lot worse, but the new guidance counselor is pretty cool, and she said it was better to reflect on how we could have behaved differently rather than spend a week in the in-school detention room.

I might've debated with her about that because Ms. Sorella, who runs in-school detention, helps everybody with their assignments, and laughs a lot, and never makes us feel bad about being in there. She's sort of a grandma kind of person. Plus, she always has food that she brings in and stashes in her mini fridge because I think she worries that some of us aren't getting enough food. Like good food. Not like junk food or stuff. Not that I'd mind. I'm not like Celeste and her little group that are always talking gluten-free and organic and going on some pricey diet named after someplace that has palm trees—you know, Mediterranean Slender this or Miami Skinny that. But Ms. S has good stuff like apples and grapes, and sometimes she bakes soda bread or banana bread or something. Actually, I know a whole bunch of kids who'd break the rules just to get assigned to Ms. Sorella's room the first day back after a holiday or a three-day weekend because then she might've made cookies or cake.

That food insecurity thing? That's not an issue I have to deal with because Mom's a good cook and has a regular job, so we usually don't have to worry about stuff, but Ms. S is right about other kids having that problem. We talked about it once, the last time I was in her room, which was because Mateo and I ditched math when there was a sub that we both don't like because he's all mean and sarcastic, and he once called a kid a "retard" and laughed, and we all kinda looked at each other because Roger, who's Mateo's best friend, his little sister Belle has Down Syndrome, and Roger did a really good article for the school paper about getting rid of the "R" word, and all his friends were like super supportive and wore t-shirts that said "Label Jars Not People." But what are you gonna do about talking back to a teacher, even if the teacher's a sub, so the next time he was in, we ditched his class.

So ditching put me in with Ms. Sorella for two days, and she told me that when she was little, kids that got free lunch were handed special cards every Monday morning—in *homeroom*, in front of *everyone*—and they had to use the cards in the cafeteria when the other kids were paying, and how embarrassing it was. She said she and her sister had to use the cards because her mom was a widow, and they didn't have a lot of money. So we agreed it's better now because all kids just have a lunchroom account, and no one knows if the account is because your parents put in money, or you get free lunch. I guess that's progress.

You know what? I could probably debate with the guidance counselor on another thing, too, which is why is she assigning writing as punishment? Yeah, like I said, she's saying it's "reflecting" but you gotta call it like you see it, and what I see is it's kinda meant to punish you for something you did. They don't ask the kids who made honor roll or won a basketball game to write essays about it.

It's true that nine kids outa ten aren't keen to fill up *three whole pages,* like I'm supposed to do here, with their reflections, but it's maybe not such a good idea to reinforce that idea. Personally, I think it would be good to make writing a reward and use something else as a punishment. The reason I think that is because this year I lucked out in my schedule and got Ms. Marshall for English, and she makes writing fun and tells us it's a way to express ourselves, and she never grades what we write but always meets with us and has lots of comments and asks us questions about our stories and has good suggestions.

She let Bradley, who can be kind of an idiot troll, write all about the video games he likes to play with his idiot troll friends, only she made him make up his own story like it was a new level of the game. She even gave him extra credit for doing drawings to go along with his story, and Bradley, even though he's an idiot troll, is a good drawer, and he did a cool picture of dragons and stuff. Ms. Marshall sorta steered him away from drawing guns by saying anybody could draw guns, but most people couldn't draw a really realistic dragon, but she bet that he could and could also describe it in what he wrote. I don't think Bradley had gotten a compliment from any English teacher *ever,* so he ended up working his butt off, and I have to say that both the picture and the story were really good.

So, I better do my reflecting now on how I could have behaved differently in the situation. I can tell you a little about Lacey, but not everything, and I don't know exactly how she's going to write about it. It's not like they put us in the same room to *confer* before we write out our three pages. It's like in those TV shows where the police put two suspects in different rooms for questioning so they can maybe trip one of them up. I don't quite get the reasoning since we're only talking about smoking and not like a heist or something.

Anyway, it was really just *stupid*. Lacey has a crush on Josie's older brother Harley who's a senior, and thinks he's super cool, but cool like from the past. Like the beatniks or something. He says he's going to be a writer, but Josie says she has her doubts about that. So we were over at Josie's one night hanging out, and—oh my god this is just so stupid— Harley kind of lounges in the doorway, and maybe he thinks Lacey is cute or something, but he asks her if he can "bum a cigarette." Lacey blushes all kinds of red, says sorry, no, and that's how the big romance begins. At least in her own head.

It took exactly *one day* before I saw Lacey had started carrying a pack of cigarettes in her handbag. Like she was hoping that at some point she'd, I don't know, bump into Harley again and be able to offer him one. I told her she was being stupid, and she sort of knew that anyway, but I could tell she was being what my mom calls equivocal.

Well, that was about a week ago, and that day in the bathroom, I was kind of double-checking on Lacey. The reason is that even if someone knows they're being stupid, and says so to their best friend, you never know how fast someone can backslide when a senior who's on his way to college shows some interest. Plus, there was that equivocal thing.

So, lo and behold—my mom always says that—she not only still had the cigarettes, she was talking like it might be cool to actually smoke herself. I told her I expected more from her, and smoking was a nasty habit, and didn't even taste good, and made your breath stink, too. And I should know because my uncle smokes, and I don't even like it when he comes in the house because his clothes smell. Like his coat will be hanging on one of the hooks in the front hall, and it reeks.

Lacey said how did I know it tasted bad when I had never smoked, and I told her I took a puff once and it was gross. My mom is *old school* about smoking. Even when my uncle is over, and even though she loves him, she's always telling him it's a nasty habit, and it's going to kill him, and if it doesn't kill him, she's going to kill him. So, anyway, when I was about ten, she gave me this smoking lecture, then she lit a cigarette and said I should take a big puff just so I'd know she was telling the truth. This was kind of her idea of a cure-in-advance that would last forever. And what happened was I took a puff and coughed my brains out and said I hated smoking and would never smoke.

So what happened in the bathroom was I was going to use my mother's cure on Lacey. I dared her to light a cigarette, puff on it, then see if she could avoid coughing. I know, I know, I know. Pretty dumb idea. So I'm really sorry, and it won't happen again. I should of acted in a different way. Especially, you know, at school. But sometimes real life happens, even when you're not in the best place for real life to happen, like at school.

I really think an appropriate punishment might be to assign me and Lacey to the detention room for a couple days. Lacey's mom isn't old school like mine, and I think Ms. Sorella could have a good talk with Lacey about a bunch of stuff. Since I've kind of used up my three pages here, is it okay if I keep going on the back? Also, can I have a copy of this to show Ms. Marshall? We're supposed to be doing a rough draft for an essay on friendship, and maybe she'll say this counts.

# Wish You Were Here

From: Owen
To: Violet
Subject: Wish you were here


It's not too late, you know. I could book you a ticket, order you a car to the airport, and pick you up here in Orlando. The cottage I rented is adorable. Straight out of the 1920s with a tiled roof and palm trees and a private little yard filled with flowers. You'd love it. Instead of getting up in the morning, pulling on your galoshes, and shoveling snow, you could wander out barefoot to the table on the patio. I'd pour you a fresh-squeezed orange juice. I'd pour it into a champagne flute. Think about it.

From: Violet
To: Owen
Subject: Thinking about it


Hmm. It said on the nightly news that it's thirty degrees in Florida. It said it's so cold that iguanas are freezing and falling from the trees. I sure hope that patio table has an umbrella. I wouldn't want you to be knocked unconscious by a giant lizard dropping from one of those palm trees. Did you know iguanas can grow up to six feet in length? Here in New England we only have to worry about snowflakes, thank you very much.

From: Owen
To: Violet
Subject: Danger from above


Only snowflakes? *Only snowflakes?* What about sleet, hail, and freezing rain? What about icicles? I'd worry more about serious injury from a six-foot icicle than a six-foot iguana. Sooooo ... I take it you're not coming?

From: Violet
To: Owen
Subject: Thank you but no thank you

No, I'm not coming. The orange juice does sound very nice, especially in a champagne flute. But I know what you'd want to do after that. Stop laughing. I'm not talking about the delightful thing we both want to do when we have time together. I'm talking about the *other* thing you'd want to do, and I'm just not going to go condo hunting with you. Not in Florida. Not in one of those segregated senior enclaves where everyone plays golf. Not that I have anything against golf. My father played on a municipal course, and walked all eighteen holes, and got lots of exercise, and had a grand old time with his buddies.

But in Florida, in some of those retirement villages, golf seems to be the be-all and end-all of everything. And it's not golf on a municipal course with old codgers who've been friends for years, and women enjoying a sport together, and high school kids using second-hand clubs and trying to learn the game. It's fancy country club golf. People wear expensive golf shoes and expensive golf clothes and drive around in expensive golf carts even when they're *not* playing golf.

And the women go to the hair salon every week, and I haven't had a professional haircut in a decade. They get their nails done, too. And Botox probably. And they've "had work done." And people smile way too much and vote conservative way too much. Not Dwight D. Eisenhower conservative like my parents. Crazy wacko conservative.

I understand this was always part of your retirement dream. Not the crazy wacko stuff, but the leave the snow and head for the sunshine stuff. But it isn't really my dream. I know we met at a rather inconvenient time for you, when your plans were kind of set. But there we are. Besides … looking at condos together? We've only been with each other for four months. *Four. Months.* Please enjoy your two weeks in Florida. Dream. Explore. Make plans maybe. If you need me, I'll be sitting here in front of a crackling fire watching the snow fall. Snow can be beautiful you know.

From: Owen
To: Violet
Subject: A calculation error

When you're over sixty, you don't measure relationships in the same way. You have to use a different mathematical formula. It's very scientific. A group of researchers at M.I.T. did the calculations and came up with the algorithm. I won't bother you with the details, but basically four months for people our age is roughly equivalent to four years for twenty-somethings. So you might wish to rethink your rather dismissive remark implying that we haven't known each other long enough to get serious.

From: Violet
To: Owen
No subject

Very funny. You're an idiot.

From: Owen
To: Violet
No subject

Better to be an idiot than a stubborn mule. P.S. I love you.

From: Owen
To: Violet
No subject

????

From: Owen
To: Violet
Subject: Greetings from the Sunshine State

Not having heard from you in 38 hours and … let me see … 16 minutes, I figured I'd just send on a breezy little note describing what I've been up to. Did you know the other nickname for Florida is The Alligator State? The state reptile is not, in fact, the iguana. It's the alligator. If you're more into amphibians than reptiles, Florida's got a good one. The state amphibian is the barking tree frog, so named because of its "raucous and explosive call." If you're talking mammals, Florida is home to some lovely ones including panthers, manatees, dolphins, and something called the Florida cracker horse. True, the state song is "Old Folks at Home" which is just as horrible as you might imagine, but no place is perfect.

Yesterday I went to look at condos. I met up with a very nice realtor who showed me some very nice homes in some very nice senior retirement villages. The units were all painted in very nice pastel colors outside, and decorated with very nice modern furniture inside, and the neighbors were all very nice, and I don't know why the hell I kept thinking about crackling fires and snowfall instead of orange blossoms and palm trees.

Yes, love can be inconvenient, but—to borrow your phrase—there we are.

From: Violet
To: Owen
Subject: A few thoughts

I'm sorry I didn't respond for more than 38 hours, 16 minutes. I had to think. So, I thought, and figured a few things out. First, you're still an idiot. Second, I freely admit I can, at times, be a stubborn mule. Third, I love you, too. And fourth—I still don't like the idea of Florida, but when I reread your notes, and saw that subject line saying, "Wish you were here," well, I don't exactly wish I was there, but I wish I could see your face. When you're back, let's talk. I think we have a lot to say.

From: Owen
To: Violet
Subject: Travel plans

I reread our correspondence, too. You said if I needed you, I could find you in front of a crackling fire, watching the snow. So, I booked a ticket, and ordered a ride from the airport. Not for you, my love. For me. I'm hoping you really do want to see my face, because I took the red eye, and I'll be there in about 15 minutes. I figure you've probably shoveled the walk by now. Retirement dreams can be revised, you know. Revised and improved. And I figured it might be fun to have cocoa in champagne flutes.

# The Bracelet

By 1939, the year she turned forty, Ella Jackson had come to possess a commanding presence. She had, as well, a tall frame, long oval face, and short brown hair that was beginning to show gray. She wore metal-framed glasses. She believed in the absolute virtue of education, hard work, and good manners. She had strong opinions and voiced them. She was persistent in arguments. She insisted that she knew the best way to handle many situations, and, to be fair, she often did. If asked her favorite color, she might have said mulberry or indigo. She was not a pastel personality. She hoped and believed that the way she had started off in life was far behind her.

Ella had been born in the last year of the nineteenth century on a small farm outside La Porte, Indiana. Ella—christened Ella Ernestine Steinbauer—was a twin, and she and her sister Elsa were the ninth and tenth children in a family that had run out of resources to support more children. As a cruel reflection of this, Elsa died before her first birthday. Elsa was not the only Steinbauer child that did not grow to adulthood. Ella's parents, Julius and Albertine, had lost two other children.

Albertine had been born in America to German-speaking parents. Julius had been brought to the United States from Prussia as a baby shortly before the beginning of the Civil War. Julius's parents could not read or write, and he himself would never learn.

In 1910, a census taker arriving at the farm recorded that the household was made up of Julius, age fifty-three, Albertine, age fifty, and their three youngest children. Fred, christened Friedrich, was sixteen, Lily was fifteen, and Ella was eleven. The other four surviving children had long since left home to make their fortunes, perhaps knowing the farm would never provide more than a hardscrabble life. Ella knew these older siblings not as playmates but as infrequent adult visitors.

When she was grown and had a family of her own, Ella rarely allowed herself to think about her childhood and the farm and how she had entered the adult world too quickly and with insufficient preparation. A little more than a year after the census taker had sat at the kitchen table, Ella was summoned to that same table from the room she shared with her older sister. Her parents needed to talk to her. Even many years later, the particulars of that talk remained garbled and unclear. Ella could recall no more than a handful of sentences. She remembered them in English, although they had been spoken in German.

"It's time for you to earn a living. They're hiring in town, at one of the big houses. They need a maid. They offer room and board."

She remembered saying something, trying to object. Even if her parents wanted her to leave school, she could stay on the farm, help with the chores. She didn't eat much. She wouldn't be any trouble.

She quickly realized she may as well have stayed silent. The decision was made. Lily was already helping with the chores. She had only attended school for a short time, and so, after years at home, knew how to cook and do the washing. And Lily was clever at sewing, something Ella had never learned. Ella was clever at school, but school didn't matter on the farm. On the farm Ella was simply another mouth to feed. As a maid, she would have a room, meals, and work. She would not be a burden.

Ella had started employment with the wealthy family the following week. Thinking back on it all—the separation from her parents and siblings, the suddenness of her departure from the farm—Ella imagined it as a metaphor. It was like having a book snatched from her hands before she had time to finish it and before she knew how the story was supposed to come out. It was a story she couldn't go back to because the book had been taken away, and she didn't know its title or where it could be found, so it was lost forever.

Yes, in the years that followed she had learned other things, things they didn't teach in school, things they didn't teach on the farm. How to clean a parquet floor, a Persian carpet, silk draperies. She learned to polish furniture, polish silver, set a table, and arrange flowers. She discovered she had a skill for nursing and cared for the wealthy family's young son when he fell ill with a fever. His grateful mother began to trust Ella's judgment and intelligence. She began to let Ella assist her with dressing and arranging her hair, then with ordering provisions, then with managing household accounts.

As she worked, Ella studied the family she served and copied their refined manners. She listened as they conversed, paid attention when they discussed the news, saw how they greeted guests and entertained. When the United States entered the Great War, she worked hard to eliminate all trace of her German accent. It would not do to be associated with the Huns. Every now and then, when she caught herself humming a German lullaby from her childhood, she would stop herself and fall silent.

Of all the lessons she learned in those years, the most important one was this: You can't live on dreams, especially dreams of what might be in the future. Hard times were right now, if not directly in your path, then waiting for you just down the street or around the next bend.

When the wealthy family moved to Illinois, to a town north of Chicago, they took Ella with them. She had learned enough about the management of a large household, to serve as something in the nature of a housekeeper. It was 1920. She was twenty-one years old.

When she met Edgar Jackson, the young man working as an athletic coach at New Trier, the large township high school, it occurred to her, for the first time in a very long time, that she might again, as she had as a child, dream of making her own decisions and having some control over her life.

The son and daughter of the family she worked for had enrolled in the high school, and Ella found herself intrigued by the giant institution and the way the school affected the community. She had loved school herself, and a large part of the heartbreak of that meeting with her parents had been the realization that she would never again be a student and never have the opportunities afforded to those that had an education.

New Trier served six well-to-do North Shore communities. It was set on acres of land not far from Lake Michigan. It had its own auditorium, a dining hall, a library, a school newspaper, a gymnasium, and a natatorium. It was the first high school in the nation to have a swimming pool. It was the first swimming pool Ella had ever seen.

So, as she continued her chores and cared for her employer's family, she asked about the school, the teachers, the assignments, the books brought home from the school library, and, after a while, the young coach that smiled at her when she came to watch a baseball game or the foot races on the athletic fields.

Edgar and Ella soon found ways to spend time together. They took walks in the park and traded stories of their childhoods. Like Ella, Edgar had been on his own from an early age. His love of sports and natural affinity for teaching had landed him a job with a summer camp in Wisconsin, then with a YMCA in Missouri. The high school coaching position had given him regular employment, a chance to stay in one place, a chance to settle down.

Ella and Edgar were married in a small ceremony at an Episcopal church. The Episcopal church was the one attended by the wealthy family Ella had worked for. To her, it symbolized not wealth, exactly, but standing. Standing as a member of a community. Standing as someone who was not a servant. Someone whose husband, while not a member of the faculty, nonetheless was known and respected as a valued employee of the high school.

Ella loved her husband and loved that she could almost fancy herself in the dream world she had created for herself in childhood, a world she had read about in books and glimpsed while in school. A daughter was born in 1924. They named her Bonnie. Another girl, Marian, followed a year later. The family lived in a pretty bungalow not far from the high school. The house did not belong to them, but they hoped that one day it would. A sum of money was paid every month to the owner of the house, an elderly man who had moved in with his daughter and her family. He had a fondness for the coach and his young family and wanted to help them, so each payment was credited toward the eventual purchase of the property. They didn't draw up a formal mortgage. The deal rested on the strength of a handshake between the two men.

Edgar built a wooden play set in the side yard. His daughters, and every other kid on the block, spent hours on the swings, the monkey bars, and the see-saw. By saving a bit of money from each week's household funds, Ella purchased a few fine things, things she thought of as elegant. She was still not adept with sewing, so her daughters' Sunday dresses and coats were store-bought. She saw goblets with gold roses on the rims in a department store display and found herself determined to get them. It took time and patience—she bought one glass at a time—but in a year she had a whole set.

In 1929 the stock market crashed. Almost overnight, things changed. Edgar did not lose his job, but money was tight. And money wasn't money. The high school paid everyone—teachers, coaches, office staff, custodians—in scrip. Some stores wouldn't take it. Some took it but not at face value.

Almost as if she had known what was coming, almost like the return of a bitter companion, life for Ella was hard again. Near the end of the month, when there was little in the house, supper might consist of soda crackers crumbled into a bowl of milk. Ella told the children the meal was a special treat. Using her formidable intelligence, ingenuity, and a strict accounting of every penny earned and spent, Ella guided the family along a precarious economic tightrope. With careful steps they walked through each week, each month, each season of the year. For a while, they maintained their balance.

Then Marian fell ill. The little girl's fever climbed, rendering her delirious, then listless. Ella tried everything she knew, everything she had learned nursing the son of the wealthy family. Nothing worked. Finally, terrified, Edgar brought the child to the hospital where she was placed in quarantine. The doctors were not sure what was wrong. They mentioned scarlet fever and the possibility of polio. Edgar was frantic, refusing to leave the hospital until he could peek through the small window in the door to the isolation ward to assure himself that Marian was still alive.

Marian's illness occasioned a horrible dilemma. Edgar and Ella could not pay the hospital and still make their monthly house payment. The elderly homeowner told them not to worry. "Take care of your child. Pay me when you can."

In time, Marian got better. She returned home weaker, but on her way to a full recovery. But soon, disaster. The man who owned the house suffered a heart attack and died. Ella found out when the man's daughter and her husband appeared at the door. It was explained that the handshake agreement held no weight under the law. It was explained that the years of steady payments meant nothing. It was explained that Edgar and Ella were renters who hadn't paid in months.

Times were tough. Pay up now, not in scrip. Pay up now or face eviction. The family relocated to a small apartment above a repair shop. Edgar began to drink.

Marian, once her health returned, was still too young to realize anything was amiss. Bonnie, however, noted every change. The bungalow and yard were gone. The swings and see-saw gone. There were no trips to the store to purchase a new dress. At night she lay awake in her room, listening to her parents fight. When a photographer came to her elementary classroom, Bonnie posed with her classmates, dutifully, solemnly, her Buster Brown haircut ornamented with a bow. The photographer was unable to make her smile.

Time passed. Perhaps one of the ultimatums Ella delivered had an effect. Or perhaps Edgar, who truly loved his wife and daughters, pulled himself away from the bottle. Because at some point the drinking stopped, a down-payment was saved, and the family started again in another bungalow on another tree-lined street.

* * *

There's something special about turning fifteen, Bonnie thought. Fifteen is *exceptional*. Fifteen is *incomparable*. She tried out a few different words, words she had seen in books, not finding quite the right term. But it didn't really matter. When you're fifteen you're old enough to get a job and earn money of your own. When you're fifteen, you're almost old enough to get married. Not that she had a boyfriend. She had never even gone on a date. She knew her classmates regarded her as something of a bookworm, a shy and studious girl who could often be found in the library, but rarely with groups of giggling friends, unlike her outgoing and popular younger sister.

Bonnie also knew that her mother worried about her older daughter's reserve. On one occasion, she had been embarrassed to overhear Mother urge Marian to include Bonnie in group outings to sports events or the movies. Marian had rolled her eyes, and Bonnie could read her sister's thoughts as clearly as if they were spoken aloud or printed in a book.

"That won't solve the problem. Besides, I can't have my older sister tag along. What would I say to my friends?"

In her mind, Bonnie answered her sister. "Don't worry. I'm not interested in spending time with a group of silly freshmen. There are more important things to talk about than who's the handsomest dreamboat in the movies and who's been seen with whom at the soda fountain. There's a war going on in Europe. President Roosevelt has talked about that. It might seem like distant thunder to you, but thunder means a storm is coming."

Bonnie was honest enough to admit to herself that these dignified comments, formulated in her head, would not be voiced. She was also honest enough to admit that maybe it would be fun, every now and then, to spend a little time at the movies and get a glass of pop at the soda fountain.

But she wouldn't need to think about that this week because this week she was going to experience a treat even more exciting than the movies. One of her cousins from the Indiana farm, a cousin she had only met a handful of times, had come for a visit, and Mother had decided the two girls could take a train into Chicago *by themselves* to see the sights. They were *fifteen,* after all.

Mother rarely spoke of her family on the farm. Her parents were gone. Her brother Fred had married, and he and his wife managed the farm. Lily had remained a spinster and helped her sister-in-law with chores and the children. But Fred had written to Ella and broached the subject of a Chicago visit for his teenaged daughter. She and Bonnie had been born the same month. They had both turned fifteen that summer.

Mother had said yes, and Kathy, her country cousin, had arrived on the bus. Bonnie had been thrilled but surprised by the whole thing. She knew the family's financial situation had stabilized, but money was still an issue. With Mother, who budgeted carefully and maintained strict control of the family's expenditures, money was always an issue.

Bonnie calculated that a number of things had brought about this unexpected excursion. Her other birthdays had never been celebrated with a special treat or a party. There hadn't been money for cake or ice cream. But she understood enough about Mother's past to know that an element of pride had played a part. Hosting Kathy, letting Bonnie take her into the city, was a way to show her siblings that she had taken her limited resources—personal courage and a few years of schooling—and earned for herself a loving husband with a regular salary, a home of her own, and two pretty daughters.

The day of the trip into Chicago arrived with warm temperatures and a sunny sky. Bonnie tried not to feel too smug as she saw Marian's resentful expression at the breakfast table and suppressed the impulse to stick out her tongue. Mother had decreed this trip would be only for the older girls. Bonnie had been to Chicago with her parents and sister before, but this was to be her first trip without an adult along.

Bonnie felt nervous, yet gloriously free, as she sat with her cousin on the commuter train as it snaked south along Lake Michigan, crossed the Chicago River, and wound past the old stone Water Tower that had survived the Great Chicago Fire. Kathy was an agreeable companion, chatty, awed by the scenes outside her window, pointing to the tall buildings, the cars, the people walking the streets in fashionable clothes.

The girls would spend the day in the Loop, the central commercial area encircled by the elevated railroad tracks. The highlight would be a trip through the glorious displays in Marshall Field & Company, Chicago's largest and most elegant department store whose flagship building covered a full block and rivaled New York's Macy's. It was a store that featured stylish home furnishings, jewelry, perfumes, and fashions from the finest designers in New York and Europe. At its heart, shoppers and tourists were beguiled by a five-story-tall atrium, surrounded by white marble balconies and crowned with a Tiffany mosaic ceiling.

It was along one of the enchanted aisles in this this magical palace that Bonnie first saw the bracelet. It was a wide bracelet made up of three strands of porcelain beads. The beads were uniform in size but had each been painted and fired in an individual pattern, with splashes of bright white and a blue so deep and vibrant it was almost purple. Both girls agreed it was beautiful. But it was also expensive. It was fifteen dollars. Bonnie knew her father's salary was less than a thousand dollars a year.

Bonnie and Kathy admired the bracelet as it sat in the glass case.

"Fifteen dollars," Kathy whispered. "That's so much money. Who could ever spend so much money for a bracelet?"

For a moment, Bonnie stayed silent. She recognized a new emotion in herself. It was a feeling of trouble, of daring, of rebellion. It was a feeling that frightened her but made her reckless at the same time.

She turned to look at her cousin then back at the bracelet. "I could buy it. I have fifteen dollars."

It had been just a moment, just before they left for the station. Mother had already given Bonnie train fare and lunch money, but in a moment of fretfulness—Bonnie had seen this happen from time to time—she had also pressed into her daughter's hands the carefully folded bills she kept for "emergencies."

Bonnie didn't even need to be told that this sum was to be safeguarded. She knew it was only to be used in a real emergency. She knew Mother would expect the full amount to be handed back upon the girls' safe return. And she knew that the purchase of an expensive bracelet could in no way be characterized as an emergency,

But the bracelet was beautiful. Even after they had moved on, walked through the magnificent department store, gazed at all its wonders, they decided to return and look at it again.

"Try it on," Kathy urged.

Bonnie, barely believing what she was doing, nodded to the salesgirl behind the counter. As the bracelet was fastened around her wrist, Bonnie heard the soft clinking sound made as the strands of beads moved against each other and felt the coolness of the porcelain against her skin.

"It's so beautiful," Kathy breathed.

Bonnie eyed her cousin. To Kathy, Bonnie's possession of the magnificent sum of fifteen dollars was simply a happy coincidence. Bonnie knew better and knew there would be terrible consequences if she purchased the bracelet. But there was that feeling of rebellion, mixed now with yearning as she regarded the blue and white beads on her wrist. She looked at the salesgirl and said what she knew were consequential words. "I'll take it."

Riding home from the city, Bonnie listened with scant attention to her cousin's chatter. Her heart thudded in her chest as she contemplated the confrontation that was sure to come. Mother was strict by nature, and hard times had made her austere. When angry she could be harsh, even frightening.

Yet Bonnie did not even try to formulate a strategy or explanation. She knew when she could get off the hook and when it was pointless to try.

As the girls entered the house, Mother came to greet them. "Did you have a good time?"

Kathy gave her a glowing smile, a thank you, and a rush of words before asking to be excused to find Marian. She had promised her younger cousin a full account of the wonders they had seen in the city.

Bonnie lingered in the small front hall. Ella studied her a moment then gestured for her daughter to follow her to the dining room. It was there, in the top drawer of the china cabinet, that Ella kept the leather coin purse that was used for the emergency money. Ella retrieved the coin purse and turned to face her daughter. It was now that the precious fifteen dollars must be returned and tucked safely away.

"Where is the emergency money?" Bonnie wasn't surprised that, somehow, Mother knew it was gone.

Bonnie remained silent for a moment, as if gathering her courage. Then it all came out in a rush. It was like diving off the high board into the deep end of the pool at the high school. "I don't have it. I spent it. I bought myself a bracelet."

She brought out the small white cardboard box, looked down at it, and held it out to her mother. There was an awful silence, as if the air had suddenly been sucked out of the room. Cheerful girlish voices sounded from another part of the house, but they may as well have been echoes from the moon.

There was a pause. Bonnie didn't move, nor did Ella. Yet Bonnie sensed that a lot was going on in that stillness, that she and her mother were part of a tableau that lacked only a narrator to explain all that was happening.

Ella felt herself caught in a complicated mix of emotions. Anger was there, and a sense of betrayal. *How could she do this? How could she not understand?* The fact that Bonnie had undoubtedly responded to the excited urgings of her cousin was not material. It was Bonnie to whom the money had been entrusted, and Bonnie who had spent it.

"The bracelet can't be returned," Bonnie stated almost defiantly.

"I know it can't," Ella snapped. "But you had no right. *You had no right.* Don't you know how hard it was to save? What if something happens and we need that money?"

"But we don't need—"

"We might … we have … we did…." Ella spoke with such ferocity that Bonnie almost stepped back.

She might have cried, but Bonnie rarely cried. Not like her younger sister. Marian was the one with the mercurial spirits, the tears, the ready laugh, the loads of friends trailing after her through the halls of the high school. Bonnie was quiet, contained, a good student, a good girl. She had never before caused her mother a moment of worry.

Bonnie looked at her mother's hands. They still held the coin purse—the purse that should have been filled with the precious, folded-up bills. Ella glanced down at it, unclicked the clasp once, then clicked it shut again, seeming almost unsure what to do next.

For the first time, Bonnie felt a spark of something very like remorse. The worn and empty coin purse in her mother's hands seemed like a sad and worthless thing, like a dead leaf or a faded flower.

"I'm so sorry," she whispered. "I know it was wrong. I know it was selfish."

Ella looked at her daughter as if seeing her for the first time. Bonnie's eyes were wide and filled with pain, but her jaw was set. Not stubborn precisely, but determined. For a moment, then two, neither said anything.

From a corner of her memory, unbidden, an image appeared in Ella's mind. She was a child again, back in the attic room in the Indiana farmhouse, studying her own reflection in the tiny round mirror hanging on the wall. It was the day she was to leave home to take up residence with the wealthy family who had hired her as a maid. Her eyes had been fearful then, in the same way her daughter's were now, her jaw determined in the same way as well. Looking at Bonnie was like looking in that mirror.

Once more Bonnie held out the box containing the bracelet. Ella reached her hand out as well, but instead of taking the box, she gently pushed it back to her daughter.

"I know what it means to want things," she said. "I know it's hard to always do without." She struggled to find the right words. "It's hard to live …."

"Hard to live how?" Bonnie asked.

"Hard to live waiting for misfortune," Ella said at last. "Maybe you won't have to do that. I hope you won't."

Bonnie was stunned. She had expected to be punished. No other result could even be imagined. The idea that her mother might understand, might let her keep the bracelet, was so unexpected that she stood rooted to the spot.

She swallowed and spoke softly. "I'll make it up to you."

Ella looked away. "Go help your sister set the kitchen table."

"Mother, I'll make it up to you."

Ella heard a note of defiance and determination in her daughter's voice. "Go help your sister set the kitchen table," she repeated. This time she looked directly into her daughter's eyes. "Put out the gold-rimmed glasses. They shouldn't just sit in the cabinet."

# At The Diner, 1942

There were only four people in the diner. Three customers and the kid behind the counter. Not surprising, perhaps. It was late, not that the concept of late usually had much meaning in New York City, a city that never sleeps. But after a month of anxious gathering and talking—in coffee shops, barbershops, dance halls, at the grocers, on front stoops, and fire escapes out back—maybe most of the day-birds and nighthawks had decided to huddle around their own radios. Maybe they'd decided to crawl into bed early, pull up the covers, and pretend for a night that bombs hadn't fallen on Pearl Harbor, and another war, so soon after the Great War, had not fallen upon the world.

In the diner, a couple sat together, cups of coffee in front of them. On a stool farther down the counter, an old man sat by himself, a fedora on his head, a folded-up newspaper at his elbow. The large panes of glass showed, for that one night of stillness, the emptiness of a city of closed doors, dark windows, red brick, and gray pavement.

The only movement came from the kid. He bent over, slid clean silverware into trays under the counter, asked the couple if they wanted more joe, wiped his hands on his apron, pushed his cap back on his head showing his short blond hair. He was enlisting in the morning. He was going to be a Navy man. His ma had cried. His pa had clapped him on the shoulder. He had their blessing.

Could he get the customers anything else? He was going to get out the white vinegar soon and clean out the urn for Mr. Kowalski who'd been swell giving him this job.

The old man in the fedora thought about the headlines in the paper. Even folded, put to the side, the newsprint seemed to demand his attention. All the news was war news. Alarms called from faraway places: Guam, Singapore, Luzon, Bataan. President Roosevelt in his State of the Union Address had said "the spirit of the American people was never higher … the Union was never more closely knit together."

The couple seemed like that, he thought. Closely knit. He had seen them before. She always dressed in something pretty, being careful with her makeup and the way she styled her long brown hair. The man she was with wore a tie, held the door for her, made her laugh. They weren't young, not like the kid. But not old, either. Just two people that maybe had found each other even though life had given them some hard knocks along the way.

He studied the couple for a moment, then looked back down at his coffee. They shoulda been somewhere other than here. Maybe swaying together to a Glen Miller tune. Maybe sharing a hot dog at Coney Island. Maybe nestled together in a movie theater watching Lon Chaney, Jr. as the Wolf Man howling at the moon.

He had seen *The Wolf Man*, brought his grandson to the Bijou. They had found seats up in the balcony, and the cigarette smoke hung around them like a haze. The picture took place at an old castle, somewhere in Europe. People walked out at night, into the darkness, and were stalked and attacked. There was a new darkness in Europe now, and it wouldn't end when the lights came up at the end of the show.

The man sitting next to the woman moved on his stool. He may have put his hand on her knee. She turned to him at last. The old man could hear her whisper.

"I know you have to go. The plans we made? They'll keep."

"I can't ask you to wait for me," her companion said. His voice was tight, full of a kind of anger. Not at her. Maybe at the world. "It wouldn't be fair."

"There's a lot of unfairness in the world right now," she said. "We both know that. We've both met up with Mr. Unfairness before. And … and to hell with that. Of course you can ask. Of course I'll wait." Very gently, she put her hand against his cheek and kissed him.

The old man felt tears sting his eyes. He unfolded the paper and began to read.

# Life of Crime

They sat on his back porch, talking, sharing stories. It had become something regular, being together like this, meeting on his back porch or sitting at the picnic table under the maple tree in her yard. There was iced tea or lemonade. Sometimes, when the August heat was intense, a cold beer.

He loved her enthusiasms, the way words spilled out of her, the unexpected observations she made, the gestures of her hands, the way she remembered lines from songs, the way she braided her hair into a long ponytail, the attention she gave to her garden, the special smile that was, perhaps, only for him.

She loved his … how to put it? His attention to the world, the things he knew, the books he read, his work in the community, what he noticed, and what he could figure out. She loved the shape of his hands, his dark hair, brown eyes, the lopsided grin that lit his features, a grin that was, perhaps, only for her.

They had, months ago now, started to talk about their lives. Where they'd traveled, wonders they'd seen, work they'd done.

"I didn't set out to lead a life of crime," she said, "and most of the time, I didn't. But sometimes shit happens."

He raised an eyebrow. "Do tell."

She laughed. "You should see the expression on your face."

"Since there's no mirror around for me to check, maybe you should describe it."

"Um, let's see. There's amusement and surprise, I would say. But I'm not sure whether the surprise is due to my admission of criminal tendencies or my use of that very mild expletive."

"I think that, as mature people, we're allowed to swear."

"You don't mean mature, you mean old."

"I mean mature."

"I don't mind the word *old*."

"I don't mind it either, but it doesn't seem to apply to you. I don't think of you that way."

"Okay, we can let that pass for now. So the surprise relates to my criminal activities."

"Since you brought up the subject, I hope you're going to provide details."

"None of my crimes are violent, you should know that from the outset."

He gave her a look. "I sort of assumed that."

She raised her chin. "Making assumptions can lead you off in the wrong direction. People make assumptions about women—older women—all the time, and it's often a mistake."

"Well, I better explain myself then. I sort of assumed you wouldn't commit a violent crime because several pieces of evidence have convinced me that violence isn't part of your nature. When that bee got into my house, and I got the fly swatter out, you crossed your arms, frowned, and launched into a lecture on the importance of pollinators."

"Pollinators are essential. We don't kill them unless absolutely necessary. And in most instances, it's not absolutely necessary."

"But it was apparently absolutely necessary that I stalk that damn insect for an hour before capturing it in a jar and setting the evil little thing free in the garden?"

"Of course it was."

"So tell me about your non-violent criminal past," he said. "Are we talking blackmail, embezzlement, or theft?"

"Theft," she said. "So there, now it's out in the open. Sometimes, when I can't think of a different solution, I steal things."

He thought about that for a minute. "Are you a modern-day Robin Hood? You've robbed from the rich to give to the poor?"

She considered. "*Sometimes*. Sometimes that's exactly what I do. Who wouldn't want to be Robin Hood? I was ten, maybe, when I first saw Robin Hood on TV. The Errol Flynn Robin Hood. My ten-year-old heart was enchanted. I wasn't *in love* with Robin Hood. I didn't want to be Maid Marian. I wanted to be Robin Hood. So sometimes, as I got older, I was. But actually, the first thing I stole I didn't give to anyone else. I kept it for myself."

"What was it?"

"A kitten."

"You stole a kitten? Aren't most kittens given away free of charge? When we were growing up, back in ancient times, weren't people handing out kittens left and right? Begging other people to take a kitten or two every time their cat had another litter. Unless, was it some kind of fancy breed like a Siamese maybe or a Persian? Not that I claim to be much of an authority on feline economic value."

"Sometimes you might want to steal something even if it's not valuable."

"Explain that," he said.

"It happens if someone has control over something when they shouldn't. They own it, and can do what they want with it, and it's the power they exert that's wrong. Sometimes even if you offer money for the item, it won't matter because it's the power they want. That's when you have to become a thief."

He took her hand. "Tell me about the kitten."

She sighed. "I named him Houdini."

He nodded. "Go on."

"You know I grew up on a farm," she said.

"In Illinois," he said.

"I'm glad you remember that. When I first moved East, I heard someone at work refer to me as 'the new girl from one of those vowel states.'"

"One of those vowel states? Oh, right. Illinois, Ohio, Indiana, Iowa."

"The Midwest. The heart of the country. Actually, each state has its own personality. And Illinois has more than one personality. Like a split personality. Chicago is right at the top of the state—"

"I know that," he said with mock dignity. "I may be a mature person myself, but I'll have you know that I placed second in our eighth-grade geography bee."

"Who placed first?"

"Belinda Faye Tucker. Smartest girl in the class." He saw her expression. "Smartest *person* in the class."

"Thank you for that amendment," she said. "But like I was saying, Illinois has a split personality. When I was growing up, everyone, *everyone*, referred to the very top of the state as 'Chicagoland,' and everything south of there was 'downstate.' I lived downstate. On a farm.

Some parts of that area are beautiful and idyllic. Like something out of a dream. Some parts are not so nice. Some parts were more sympathetic to the Confederacy than the Union. There was a big Klan presence there for a long time. But I'm getting away from the story. My first crime."

"You look troubled."

"It's not a happy story. But I learned from it."

"Do you want some more iced tea first?"

"Not now. Maybe when I'm done confessing, we can have more tea. Or a beer. Well, here goes. I grew up on a farm. Our neighbors were other farm folks. We had chickens and cows. We grew corn and had apple orchards. Farm folk, most of them anyway, take good care of their animals. Most of their animals. But not all. There were always cats around, mostly feral. They'd move into the barns and catch mice and have kittens. Lots of kittens."

"I'm getting the picture. It wasn't a time when people would bring them to the vet to be neutered then placed for adoption."

"No, it wasn't. If there were too many cats and too many kittens, some people would drown them. So that's the reality of the time and place. Some of the people that did that, it was meant to be kind. But drowning an animal isn't a fast and easy way to go."

He was still holding her hand. He could feel it shaking, so he laced his fingers with hers.

"You rescued a litter of kittens. You stole them when they were going to be drowned?"

"No. That's what I wish I had done. That's what I learned I should have done. It was summer. I was at the pond. There was a pond between our farm and the next one over. It was a nice place with some trees for shade. I liked to swim there. A lot of kids did. Or just sit there with a book.

"One day a boy from the next farm showed up. He had a sack, and it was moving, and I could tell what it was and what he was going to do."

"Go on."

"The boy was Randall. He was older than me, maybe fourteen, fifteen. He was trouble. He had a mean streak. I knew that much, but I didn't know much more. Back then I didn't understand the complexity of behavior that is cruel. I just knew that he teased other kids at school and got into fights."

"What happened?"

"He came up to the edge of the pond. And then he saw me sitting under one of the trees. I don't even remember why I was there that day or what I was doing. I hadn't put on my swimsuit. Maybe I was just daydreaming, staying out of the sun. After he saw me, he held up the sack, and I could see it moving, and he was close enough that I could hear them."

She swallowed.

He didn't say anything, just waited until she was ready to go on.

"I called out to him. I said, 'Randall, give them to me. I'll take them home and take care of them.' He looked at me, and he got this expression of, I don't know, contempt I guess, and made a point of ignoring what I was saying. Like I wasn't there. Then I offered to *buy* the kittens. I told him I had saved money from my allowance, and I would buy the kittens, but I'd have to run back to the house and get my money. I used to keep it in a shoebox under the bed. 'Just wait ten minutes,' I said. 'I'll be back in ten minutes.'"

"And?"

"He laughed at me. I could see he was tempted by the money, but he wanted something more than the money. He wanted the power in the situation. Over the kittens. Over me. He cocked his head to the side and pursed his lips like he was considering my offer. He kept his eyes on my face like he was thinking about what I had said. Then he smiled and threw the bag into the middle of the pond.

"I was in shock for a second, but then I scrambled to my feet and jumped in the water. I was a good swimmer, fast, even though I was wearing shorts and a tee shirt. And then, then he started screaming at me. His first words to me were those screams. 'Those are mine. Don't you dare!' He started swearing and waving his arms around. But he couldn't stop me. He didn't follow me into the water. Maybe he didn't know how to swim."

"Did you get to them?"

"Yes. Yes and no. The bag wasn't tied very tightly, and he hadn't put rocks in there to make it sink. I got to the bag and one kitten was already struggling out. I got him and got hold of the top of the bag and swam to the other side of the pond, away from Randall. I turned the bag upside down, and some of the kittens got out and ran off. But I don't know if all of them did. Randall started around the pond, coming after me. My clothes were drenched, but I picked up the bag and held onto that one kitten and ran. He didn't follow onto our farm, but I heard him, still screaming. He called me a thief and a bitch."

She looked over at him. "That's how it began. My life of crime. I stole a kitten by jumping into a pond. A noble effort. But inept. I saved some of them, but maybe not all."

He took her hand and brought it to his lips. "Do you want that beer now?"

"That would be most welcome. Thank you. And thank you for listening."

"As long as you're willing to talk, I'm willing to listen."

"As long as you're willing to listen, I'm willing to talk. My life of crime began with a kitten. After the kitten, every now and then, there were other things that needed doing, needed stealing."

"Sometimes, as you noted, shit happens."

"It does. But sometimes good things happen, too. Why don't we have a beer, and I'll tell you everything. As long as you're interested."

"I am. But tell me first, was Houdini a good cat?"

She smiled. "The best. Fierce, and arrogant the way some cats are, but happy to sit on your lap on a winter's day whenever you needed company."

He nodded, satisfied. "I'll get the beer."

# Big Brother

The kid and the teenaged boy sat on the wall that surrounded the playground. The teen had a baseball glove in his hand and a ball. The kid's feet didn't reach the ground, and periodically he'd kick his legs back and forth, his heels hitting the stone.

"Last year, when we met at the community center, did you pick me for your little brother because you got there late, and I was the only one left?"

"No, we were supposed to be paired up anyway. It's not like picking people for a dodgeball team in gym class where everyone stands around waiting to get chosen, and somebody always gets picked last."

"Did kids really get picked for teams that way in the old days when you were young? Like I've seen it in some of those old TV shows, with the gym teacher's favorites being made dodgeball captains, and they pick all their friends and all the good athletes, one by one, until the only ones left are kids with no friends and no athletic ability, and their self-esteem is like totally destroyed in five minutes."

"Yeah, it happened that way. And then the kids that got picked last would get pounded in the game. Just to make their humiliation complete. It wasn't, like, fair, but that's the way it was. Everybody, well most people, just went along with it."

"You sound like you're speaking from experience. Not from experience being one of the last kids picked. But like you saw it happen to other kids."

"Of course I'm speaking from experience. I'm older than you. I've seen some pretty medieval stuff that youngsters like you have never gone through."

"You're not that much older than me. I'm nine. You're eighteen. That's only nine years difference. That's less than a *decade*, which isn't really very long, when you think about it. Like when you think about dinosaurs and Ancient Egypt and stuff."

"You haven't been alive for a decade."

"You've only been alive for *one* decade, plus eight years."

"Good calculating there. Did they teach you that in that special, fancy, super-smart-kids math class you take?"

"Ha, ha. Very funny."

There was a pause when neither of them said anything for a while. The teen took the ball and slapped it into the mitt a couple of times, then he spoke.

"I didn't pick you because you were the only one left when I got there."

"When you got there *late*."

"I know I got there late, but I haven't been late ever since. It was only that one time, and that was a long time ago."

"It was one year and two months ago. And I was *traumatized*. And kids remember trauma for a long time. There I was in the cafeteria at the community center, and all the other kids had been matched up with their big brothers and big sisters, and they were sitting at tables and playing board games and looking at comic books and stuff, and there I was, odd man out."

"You're not a man. You're a kid. And I got there, didn't I? And you don't like board games and comic books anyway."

"I like Batman."

"Okay, except for Batman." The teen looked over at the kid then away. "I didn't ever tell you why I was late. I thought maybe I should do that now because, you know, we're not going to be able to see each other so much once I start college in the fall."

He shot another look at the kid. "Now, don't look that way. We're still going to see each other, right? I've already got tickets for us to go to that Yankees game. And now that you've got your own cell phone, we can talk whenever you want."

The kid kicked his feet back and forth for a while then started talking again. "You were going to tell me why you were late that first day."

"It was because I wasn't supposed to be there. I wasn't supposed to be a big brother. I was kinda what you might call a last-minute replacement, like on a baseball team when someone's pulled outa the game, and you have to send someone else in."

"Who got pulled out?"

"Richard Hanover. He plays baseball, too, and got a sports scholarship that he doesn't really need because his dad is pretty rich. He kinda pulled himself out. He had signed up to be a big brother, but then decided to do that Mighty Man Charity Challenge instead. That was a one-shot deal, but there was going to be a lot of press coverage, so it would look just as good on his college application resume in the *What kind of community service do you do?* category. Plus there were a lot of cute girls that were going to be there."

"So, I was supposed to be your community service project? For like your college application?"

"Sorta. The guidance counselor told me I was a pretty good ballplayer, which kinda balanced out my so-so grades—I'm not a Brainiac like you. But he said it would help my college applications if I stopped being a self-centered asshole and did something worthwhile, and they needed another big brother. So I should volunteer. And if I didn't volunteer, he might not go the extra mile to help me collect my letters of recommendation and fill out the forms and stuff."

"Guidance counselors aren't supposed to threaten kids and call them assholes."

"Wait till you get to high school."

"And you're not supposed to use words like that in front of impressionable kids like me."

"You use worse."

The kid giggled then spoke. "Soooo … you were kinda the kid picked last when they were putting together the group of big brothers and big sisters. Must've been a new experience for you. Like I bet you were never really picked last in sports stuff."

"I wasn't. But I've been last in lots of other stuff. Stuff you won't have to worry about. I flunked algebra in my sophomore year and had to go to summer school."

The teen looked over at the kid and nudged his arm. "You know why I got you your own cellphone, right? The real reason?"

"Yeah, yeah, you told me. So I can call whenever I want. You told me that." He hesitated, then went on. "And it makes things a little better, and my mom said to be sure to thank you. So thank you."

"Well, that's the real reason, but only *part* of the real reason."

"What's the other part of the real reason?"

"I got you that phone so *I* could call *you* whenever *I* wanted. Because, you know, these days when we do stuff, talk about baseball and stuff, and days when you come to my games with your mom and cheer me on, it's been, um, real nice. And I like hearing about your stuff, too. All that science stuff you do, and I'm real proud of you about that math class."

"You're going to miss me, aren't you? That's what you're saying, isn't it?"

"That's what I'm saying."

"It's going to be okay. We can still be friends. I'm not going anywhere."

"You betcha we can still be friends. Good friends. Friends for life. You're my little brother, like for real. But you're wrong about one thing, kid. When you said you're not going anywhere? That's the part that's wrong. You're going to the stars some day. As high as you want. As far as you want. And I'm going to be there cheering you on."

# Housesitting

Edwina wasn't sure why she had agreed to this crazy idea, but here she was, struggling to get into a ridiculous late-Victorian-era outfit. The shirtwaist and long skirt would have looked completely appropriate in about 1901 but was fussy as all hell in the twenty-first century. She finished up the buttons, smoothed the skirt, then began work on her hair. She was going to try to pin it up like a Gibson Girl, and she had a variety of hair pins and a celluloid clip at the ready for the task.

This is what I get, she thought, for taking this job at the Oxford-Morrow House, the only building in her little corner of Connecticut that had been put on the national register of historic places by the United States Department of the Interior. This is what I get for falling in love with, and moving in with, Winston Morrow Bailey, head of the Oxford-Morrow Trust which held, as its mission, the preservation of the Gilded Age mansion and the education of the public about the history of the era in which it had been built.

"Why can't a museum docent just be a docent?" she had asked Winston when he first explained the housesitting idea. "Why can't we escort visitors around the mansion, answer questions, keep children from handling the exhibits, sell souvenirs in the gift shop, and bid them all a fond farewell when five o'clock rolls around. You know, close the curtains, run around with a dust cloth and vacuum cleaner, polish the plaque designating us a landmark, then lock up, walk home, zap something in the microwave, and watch the ballgame. Why this idea of housesitting in a house that's really a museum."

"But housesitting in a historic home is a brilliant idea," he had replied. "That conference I went to on tourism and the management of historic homes devoted an entire afternoon to the housesitting concept and its connection to the idea of reenactment. There were panelists who were experts on Sturbridge Village, the Shelburne Museum, Hearst Castle, the Lockwood-Mathews Mansion, and Mystic Seaport."

"You told me all about it," she said. "Endlessly. It's convinced me that maybe you should bring a chaperone to the next conference you go to. Someone to look after you and keep you tethered to the practical and possible."

"I'll agree to that if you'll agree to be the chaperone. You can tether me to anything you like, but might I suggest the feather bed in the east wing? It's very comfortable, and I could recount the history of tick mattresses, and you could, um, keep me company. Did you know featherbeds were so valuable, they were listed in people's wills? It takes fifty pounds of feathers to make one decent mattress."

Edwina laughed and rolled her eyes.

"But look," he continued, "having someone live at an historic house, live like people lived fifty, or eighty, or a hundred years ago serves the educational mission of the site. A house sitter who's here twenty-four hours a day—for a week, or two weeks, or a month—will know what it's really like to inhabit a past time period. They did a version of this at Beechwood in Newport, Rhode Island. When a tourist bought a ticket for a tour of the mansion, they were treated like a member of 'the Four Hundred,' New York's most elite social group. They were greeted by John Jacob Astor IV. It was like they'd gone back in time. It was living history."

"Tourists don't buy tickets for Beechwood," she pointed out. "Not anymore. Not since it was bought by that billionaire. And when they did, they were greeted by an *actor* who went home at night and slept in his own bed. And if they really did go back in time, they would do well to tell young Mr. Astor to forgo passage on the *Titanic*. And Beechwood has thirty-nine rooms and is surrounded by other Gilded Age mansions, and Newport has that lovely beach, and the cliff walk, and beautiful restaurants right on the water. The Oxford-Morrow house only has nineteen rooms, and that's if you count the pantry, and it's surrounded by poultry farms."

He laughed. "But you'll do it, won't you? We can build a whole marketing campaign around the idea. When school groups come you can talk to them about what nineteenth-century plumbing was like, and how to cook on a cast iron stove, and how music sounds when it's played on a gramophone. I'll help you. The whole staff will help you."

"The 'whole staff' consists of you, me, the board members of the trust who have a lot of other things to do, the volunteers from the senior center, and the occasional high school or college kid that likes history. And—"

"And what?"

"Why don't you do the housesitting yourself? You've been a reenactor, and I know you did some acting in college. No one knows more about this house and the Gilded Age than you do, and that includes a few of the history professors I had at college. And no one loves this museum more. I've seen the way you greet the groups that come to tour the house. And you're wonderful at interviews and talks to libraries and college groups. You actually know how to operate that cast iron stove. I'm the queen of carry-out."

"I've done a bit of this kind of thing," he replied, "when I first acquired the house. Back then, you know, it wasn't even open to the public on a regular basis. It was badly in need of restoration. It had been a long time since anyone understood the importance of structures like this, the importance of learning about the past. When I first got here, I spent a week in the house, just moving through the rooms, trying to get a feel for the time period and the lives of the people who lived here. Trying to … go back to that era, I guess you'd say."

"Then why not continue with that now? Why do you want *me* to be the house sitter?"

When Winston didn't answer, she had turned from her perusal of a stack of new brochures to study him. He'd had a funny expression on his face. And not much of an answer. It was unusual for Winston to not have much of an answer.

"I think the house will speak to you," was all he'd said.

* * *

Edwina examined herself in the oval cheval glass mirror that stood next to the carved wardrobe. She had achieved moderate success with her Gibson Girl hairstyle. *The house will speak to me.* Indeed, she thought to herself, and drew a deep breath. It occurred to her that drawing a deep breath was only possible because she had refused to wear a corset. Authenticity in reenactment was important, she had explained to Winston, but the ability to breathe was paramount.

"Besides, corsets were on their way out by the end of the nineteenth century," she'd said. "They would eventually be replaced by girdles, then girdles went out the window, and there was a lovely period of freedom with, you know, plain old underwear or plain old nothing at all. Sadly, the fashion industry is reintroducing confinement. Now it's called *shapewear*."

She noticed his expression.

"Okay, this conversation is over," she said.

He was trying, not very successfully, to keep a straight face. "Hey, I agree with you," he said. "My great-grandmother was a suffragist and a proponent of women's sports. She wore bloomers for bicycle riding and said they were the most comfortable thing she'd ever worn."

"How do you know that?" she asked.

"You know, family lore, stories I heard."

She narrowed her eyes. "You told me you weren't raised here. You told me you had no idea you were related to the Morrow family until that lawyer found you and said you were the sole remaining heir after old Mrs. Morrow died."

"About those family stories … sometimes, like I said, the house speaks to you."

She looked at him skeptically. "Well, if you agreed with me on the corset, why didn't you say so at the get-go?"

He grinned. "It was fun hearing you talk about ladies' underwear."

Even without having to don a corset, the housesitting experience— staying by herself in the rambling Beaux Arts mansion—had taken some getting used to. She wasn't alone during the day, of course. The mansion hosted the usual tourists and school groups, and Edwina found she rather enjoyed appearing in costume, in her role as a visitor from the past, describing life in the house in the 1890s. At night, she knew Winston was no more than a stone's throw away in their modern furnished residence out back in what used to be the caretaker's cottage.

But Winston had told her he wasn't going to visit her after closing time and would do his best to stay out of sight so he wouldn't "pull her back to modern times." For the same reason they had decided that reminders of the present should not be around or should stay out of sight. That meant no television and no laptop. Her phone was available in case of an emergency, but she kept it in a drawer and out of her hands. No radio, no newspapers, no magazines, or modern books.

At night, it wasn't creepy exactly—she was familiar with and confident in the modern security system that protected the entire site—but still. The mansion was a space intended to be filled with people—in the library and conservatory, the morning room, sunroom, and dining room. There should be people in all the bedrooms and children in the nursery and maids and a cook and a butler. And yet there she was as the sun set at night, all by her lonesome.

She had taken to humming to herself, although, mindful of what this housesitting experience was supposed to teach her, she stayed with songs popular in the 1890s like "The Band Played On" and "Sidewalks of New York." From the mansion's library she selected *The Time Machine*, published in 1895, and Bram Stoker's 1897 novel, *Dracula*. One night she pulled out the Holmes stereoscope and spent an enchanting few hours viewing stereo cards showing 3-D scenes of Lake Superior, the Rocky Mountains, and Indian teepees at an encampment in Colorado.

It was at about the ten-day mark—Edwina had agreed to a month of housesitting—that the house first spoke to her. Not the house itself, to be specific. It was one of the others. One of the women who lived there.

After escorting the last of the day's tourists out the door, Edwina had started singing to herself, rather loudly. It was "Shine on Harvest Moon," a hit from the early 1900s, and she got to the line about having no lovin' since April, January, June, or July.

"Ain't that a sad story," she said aloud as she finished the song. Then, from the kitchen, she heard someone giggle.

Her first reaction was to be startled, then curious, then a little alarmed. Not that she was frightened by a giggle, but it occurred to her that maybe a teen had snuck inside as a prank, or a child had decided to play hide-and-go-seek and was even now being frantically sought by worried parents.

Then she saw the woman standing just inside the kitchen gesturing her to come forward. It was a woman dressed in an ensemble similar to her own, her hair pulled up and pinned in the same manner. She was older than Edwina, however, probably in her fifties.

Edwina knew who she was, although she couldn't be who she was. Edwina had seen her portrait in the library. It was Theresa Susan Morrow, suffragist and—if Winston was to be believed—bicycle rider. Edwina's mind both accepted and rejected the idea. Winston must have hired someone, an acting friend or someone from his old reenactor group. He must have found someone to keep her company and help her "experience the early 1900s."

The woman gestured again, and Edwina walked forward. "Come into the kitchen, dear," the woman said. "We can be comfortable there and have a nice chat. Winston warned me you're a very practical and down-to-earth person, so I know you'll have quite a few questions, and you'll want to make sure I'm not a charlatan or a play-actor. So we can address that first if you like. I'm confident you'll figure out some way to verify who I am. Some sort of test. I suppose I could disappear and reappear or something like that, or you could ask me questions that only I would know the answer to.

"But while you consider that matter, let's have a conversation about what you might want to learn about my *time period*. Winston is a dear boy, I'm so proud of him, but he's very focused on what he calls 'artifacts' and what I call the practical and mundane. The last time we met he asked a whole series of questions about tick mattresses, how they were made and how long they would last and what they were worth. I told him everything I knew, but really, is this what history is all about? I suggested, very gently, that he was always welcome, but it might be a good idea to send you along to do a bit of housesitting, and now here you are."

Edwina smiled weakly. She wasn't sure what to say, so it took her a minute to respond. Finally she managed. "Is there something *you* wish to talk about? You're right that history is more than artifacts, but are there any topics you want to … expand upon?"

The old woman smiled. "Oh, there's so much we must discuss. There's women's suffrage, of course. Winston has already filled me in on the Nineteenth Amendment, but I gather there are still rather striking areas of inequality. I could tell you about the women who set up settlement houses and those ladies who became muckrakers, and—"

"Bloomers," Edwina said. "Winston told me you wore bloomers and loved them."

Theresa's eyes twinkled. "I did. I do. It's ridiculous to expect women to wear a long skirt when operating a bicycle. Did you know both Elizabeth Cady Stanton and Susan B. Anthony advocated for women riding bicycles? And did you know that some doctors claimed a woman's sexual health was at risk if she sat on a bicycle seat? They weren't concerned about 'health' of course. It was a patriarchal view of morality. It was about control. But come, my dear, let's have a cup of tea, and you can work out how to prove I am who I say I am, and then we can talk about history. And bicycles. And bloomers."

Edwina considered. Yes, there were tests she could do, things only Edwina knew about the house and its history, things that she hadn't told Winston, little details that seemed unimportant. Winston, too, had that kind of knowledge. Sometimes, at night, when they had time, they would share their little discoveries. Winston had told her about finding a man's cufflink in the back of an old dresser. She had commented on a tiny hole she'd noticed in one of the silk brocade draperies. It had been mended so cleverly that it was essentially invisible, the stitches blending in perfectly with the fabric's floral design. She could present this woman, whoever she was, with a list of questions, things only Theresa Susan Morrow would know.

But somehow, Edwina knew the woman in front of her could answer all the questions, pass every test. There was something about her look, her voice, her manner of standing, the expression on her face. It was like a movie, but not like a movie. A dream, but not like a dream.

Edwina drew a deep breath, squared her shoulders, and stepped into the kitchen.

# Fortune Teller

I don't expect you to believe me on this one, but whenever I've had a few drinks and think about it, it brings a smile to my face. Heck, it brings a smile to my face even when I haven't had a few drinks, so it may operate the same way on you. The only trouble with trying to tell it is that so many years have passed that I'm not a hundred percent sure about every detail. I know some women think you're supposed to remember every detail about this kinda thing, but I think I remember the feeling more than the details. That's what's important, isn't it? The feelings I had then, and I still have now.

As for the details, well, the big stuff I know, but some of the little stuff might've gone and got mixed up with something I read or heard about or saw in a movie theater somewhere. A movie theater ... yeah, that's the right comparison. It feels like that. Like when the lights have gone down in one of the old movie houses, one that has ornamental decorations and a balcony and box seats on the side and a red velvet curtain that opens just before the picture comes up. You feel something magical is happening.

Anyway, I'll just tell you the story, and why it makes me smile, and you can make of it what you will. There's truth at the heart of the story, and that's what really matters.

The story starts back about 1946. It was just after the war when a lot of young men were looking around and all of a sudden realizing they had made it through, had survived Midway or Iwo Jima or Normandy. A lot of women were looking around, too, and maybe their sweethearts or husbands were coming home, and maybe they weren't, and they had to figure out their lives in a different way. My neighbor Mrs. Veniti was one of the ladies on our street that had to do that different way kind of figuring. Her husband hadn't made it back from the Pacific.

Mrs. Veniti was a little on the older side to be a war widow, but the Selective Service Act in '40 drafted men up to age forty-five, and Mr. Veniti was forty-three, and anyway, he volunteered right after Pearl Harbor. When he died, those first few months into the war, that left Mrs. Veniti alone with the kids—Nicky, who was fifteen and played basketball, and Carolee, who was thirteen and liked to draw. Plus Mrs. Veniti had her mother-in-law, Nona Veniti, who lived with them. On top of that was the fact that Mrs. Veniti had a bad leg on account of polio when she was a kid, and she walked with a limp, dipping down to the side with every step.

The end result of this was that the Venitis knew they were going to have to figure out some way to supplement their income. So they had a family talk. Nona Veniti was the one who figured it out. She and her daughter-in-law got on like a house on fire, which isn't always the case with mothers-in-law and daughters-in-law. But what I've learned about women is that what we men think is the case often isn't the case at all.

Well, before you know it, there was a sign up at the Venitis to ring the bell in the back for fortune telling. "The back" was their back sunroom which had its own set of steps to the backyard. The Venitis, like a lot of folks at that time, had a nice little set up in their yard with a chicken coop and a rabbit hutch and a grape arbor. There was a bench, too, underneath a big oak tree that added shade. Customers, if there was more than one, could sit on the bench and wait their turn to see Nona Veniti.

Yep, you got that right. Nona was the fortune teller. She would do card reading and interpret the lines on people's palms and sometimes gaze into a crystal ball and call up the ghosts of people who had passed. Apparently, Nona had done something along this line back in the old country before she and her husband had come to the U.S. and landed at Ellis Island. Papa Veniti had been an organ grinder and had a monkey, and he'd stand in the square on market days. If you gave a coin to the monkey, you could get your fortune told. Nona would wear a pretty peasant dress and stand with her husband—she was young and good-looking then—and take the customer's hand and tell them they would find luck or a livelihood or love. All the important stuff. All the stuff people really need.

So, the Venitis sewed some curtains from dark blue material printed with little white stars and put them up in the sun porch. They set up a wood card table and covered it with a tablecloth made from the same material as the curtains. And before you knew it, a lot of the folks from the neighborhood, and even from across town, were dropping by and placing their dollar bills in an emptied-out goldfish bowl that Nicky set out by the door.

Carolee helped too. She had finished high school by then and made a little money by doing hairdressing and manicures for some of the ladies in town. In between that, she put on a head scarf made from that same starry fabric and carried a little basket around the neighborhood. The basket held cards that she drew herself advertising the fortune-telling business, and Carolee would drop them in people's mailboxes.

It was a different time. A hard time *and* a hopeful time. The Venitis weren't the only family who had lost someone. Some families had lost more than one. But still, there were people, lucky ones, who had made it through and could look ahead. There were young men who would go to college on the G.I. Bill and could buy a home with no money down. In hard times and hopeful times, a fortune teller can get a lot of business.

I'll bet you want to know if I ever put a dollar in the fishbowl and had my fortune told. Well, I did. I figured it was a way to help out the Veniti family. They were good people, good neighbors. And I have to say I was curious. Sometimes I'd come home from a day at the railyard where I was working back then and see two or three ladies sitting on the bench in the Venitis yard, chatting away, waiting their turn to see Nona. Sometimes a man would join them. Even, every now and then, a younger person. So one day—it had been a long day—I checked my wallet, saw that I had a dollar bill, and took my place on the bench.

There was a young lady on the bench with me, and she got called in right quick. What would happen was that Carolee would come outside and nod her head in your direction which was a signal that it was your turn to go in. Sometimes, if the person on the bench was old, she'd hold out her hand or take the person's arm to kind of guide them along and give them support.

The young lady that I'd shared the bench with had been sort of sad looking, not crying exactly, but her face had a defeated expression. It wasn't as bad as the expressions you'd see during the war when there'd be one of those boys carrying a telegram to the door. It was more like a young woman's unhappiness that maybe came from not having money for a new dress or a night out at the pictures, or maybe from finding out her beau was stepping out with someone else.

Don't get me wrong. I'm not playing down anyone's unhappiness for any reason. Man's or woman's. If I'd learned anything during the war, it was how complicated unhappiness could be. It could come in all sizes, that's for sure, and you can't know what else in someone's life might be playing a role in how they feel.

Like me, for instance. I'd been one of the men that didn't get in the army, not for lack of trying. Sure, I'd gone to the recruiting station like most every man I'd known, even though I was pretty sure what would happen.

It was because of my hand. I hadn't always worked at the railyard. When I finished high school, this was before the war started, I joined up with the CCC, the Civilian Conservation Corps. I thought this was the best bet for someone like me. I'd be working five days a week, have a place to sleep and three squares a day. You'd get thirty dollars every week with twenty-five being sent home for your folks. The only family I had left at that point was Pappy, but the money helped keep a roof over his head.

It worked great for a while. Our crew was in Black Rock State Park up by Watertown. I did six months and reupped for another. Then we were clearing land for a road using not much more than picks and shovels, and the fella next to me gets frustrated and swings his pick wrong just when I'm reaching down to pull a rock outa the dirt. I don't like to think about it, but that's how I ended up with two fingers gone from my right hand. The index finger and the middle finger are gone, and there wasn't anything the doc could do about it.

The guy who swung his pick wrong gets canned, but I'm out too. My right hand was the one I wrote with and used. It took a lotta months of practice and training my own hands before I didn't feel embarrassed about how I did things. Course I could use my left hand for lotsa things like doing up buttons or eating with a fork. But other stuff took time to figure out. I could print if I took it nice and slow, but using a lot of tools or signing my name in script was something else.

The men at the recruiting station halfway appreciated that I wanted to enlist and halfway didn't want me to waste their time. So I ended up 4-F and spent the war at the railyard. That's one lesson I had in the complicated business of being unhappy. I know there are some who would say that being 4-F meant that Pappy never had to answer the door and see a boy with a telegram standing there. But it wasn't something I wanted or looked for. And the way my hand was—that was something that was going to stay with me forever.

All these things were kind of floating in my brain as I sat on the bench under the oak tree in Mrs. Veniti's yard. After a little while, the door to the back porch opened and the young lady who'd been with me on the bench came out, and she's different. She had a smile on her face, and she looked a little bit more hopeful. When she headed off along the pathway to the front of the house, I swear she had a skip in her step.

Carolee came out, and I was surprised she didn't just nod and wave her hand for me to come in. Instead, she came down the porch steps and walked over to the bench and held out her hand.

"I don't need help," I said, and I said it a little rough because I was thinking she's treating me like one of the old folks or a cripple.

Carolee closed her lips tight and gave a little huff, like she knew that already and didn't need me to tell her. She brushed back a curl of black hair, and I noticed she had dark brown eyes the color of coffee, or maybe a bar of chocolate.

Then she held her hand out again and said, "Nona said I'm to hold your hand, the right one. She said it's important for your fortune." She looked at me again like she's making sure I understand what I'm supposed to do. When I didn't move, she reached over and took my hand in hers and very gently gave it a tug. "You can trust what Nona tells you," she said in a real quiet voice. "She knows things."

I have to say, the feeling of Carolee's hand in mine almost knocked me over. It was like holding a little rabbit or a bird, something wild but something that trusted you at the same time. It made me realize that it had been years since I had touched anyone with that hand—or anyone had touched me. I looked at Carolee and our eyes met, and I wondered if, to her, I was the one like that rabbit or bird.

Hand in hand, we walked up the back steps and into the sun porch. Nona was sitting at the table with her eyes closed, and I wondered if she was asleep. There were two chairs at the same table, so we sat down. Carolee still had hold of my hand, and it sounds a little strange, but it wasn't awkward anymore.

Nona wasn't asleep, and as soon as we were seated, she opened her eyes and smiled. Carolee said something to her in Italian, and even though I don't really know the lingo, I could tell she was asking Nona if she wanted the crystal ball. Nona held her hand up in a gesture that I could tell meant no, then turned to me.

"Thank you for coming, Mr. Dobransky," she said, almost like she was having a little tea party, and I showed up. "When Carolee said you were on the bench, it made me very happy. Now we will take a look and see why I feel this and where your fortune and happiness can be found."

With that, she very carefully took my hand, the right one, the one Carolee had been holding, and opened it and laid it on the table with the palm up. I was thinking it was an ugly thing for her to see, and for Carolee to see, but neither of them seemed upset in any way. Nona pointed with her finger and began to trace the lines on my palm, the one that curves down around my thumb and the two that cut across under my fingers, the two fingers I have left there. I could feel Nona's touch, and again it was a strange feeling, but not a bad one.

Nona said something to Carolee, and I saw them both nod. It's almost like she was teaching Carolee how to do palm reading. Then Nona smiled at me and said, "Very good. This is very, very good."

Next she did something that I didn't expect, and maybe Carolee didn't expect, and maybe even Nona herself didn't expect because it seemed spontaneous. Here is what she did. She took Carolee's hand, her right one, and opened it and laid it on mine in the same position. So Carolee's palm is up, and the back of her hand is against my palm. Her thumb and little finger and ring finger rested on mine, and her other two fingers filled the space where I just have scars.

Then Nona traced the lines on Carolee's hand, and both of us could see how much they were the same as the ones on mine.

We stayed that way for a while. Then Nona tilted her head toward us and spoke Italian again, and Carolee said what we were both supposed to do then was pick a card from the fortune telling deck. The deck of cards that was on the table wasn't like a regular deck of cards like you could use to play a game of gin. It was a deck that I'd guess you'd say was homemade.

I looked at Carolee. "Did you make the cards?" I asked. I remembered Carolee before the war, when she was still young, coloring pictures with crayons, and sometimes using chalk to cover the sidewalks with flowers and clouds and fish and birds and imaginary creatures.

She nodded. "Nona told me what the pictures needed to be, and I drew them." Then Carolee said to me, "You go first."

So I picked a card from the very middle of the deck and handed it to Nona who turned it over. The picture on the card showed a road that's coming out of a forest and heading up a hill, and on either side of the road there are fields with flowers in them.

Nona nodded her head yes, like it showed her something she expected.

"Now you," I said to Carolee because by now the fortune telling was about the two of us, and though it should've felt strange, it didn't feel that way at all.

I was surprised when Carolee shook her head. "You pick for me," she said. She must have seen I was confused because she explained. "Nona has told me that for any of this to work, you have to believe it. If not all the way, at least part of the way. If I pick the card, you might one day wonder if it was all set up that way, like a trick. Nona doesn't do tricks. I don't do tricks. We just try to see if there's something there to be seen."

I could see what she was trying to convey. So I picked a card for her, one from near the top of the deck and handed it to Nona without looking at it.

Nona took the card and looked at it and smiled, and maybe she had tears coming into her eyes, the happy kind of tears. She turned the card over and placed it on the table. The picture showed hands—a man's hand and a woman's hand—and the fingers were laced together.

Nona repeated what she said before. "This is good. This is very, very good."

What happened after that is that she explained it all—our fortunes—and all the complicated lessons Carolee and I might learn in the future, might learn together, perhaps—the complicated lessons on how to have hope, how to be happy. That day on the sun porch I heard my fortune and found my future—a future of luck and a livelihood and love.

# Billina

An alien invasion would be welcome about now, she thought. The appearance of a skyful of flying saucers would provide a good excuse to leave. Billina felt hideously out of place at this event, and it was an *event* despite being billed as "just a casual little backyard neighborhood barbecue, drop in *whenever*."

Connecticut's idea of a little neighborhood barbecue—at least this Gold Coast, big-money part of Connecticut—wasn't at all like a barbecue in her little town in Kansas. For one thing, neither Myra nor Derek, the couple that had invited her, were actually standing at the grill since there was a uniformed chef for that. He was doing something with skewers. Also, they were not actually in a "backyard" since most of the beautifully groomed area behind the house was covered by an expansive deck and a wide stone patio surrounded by large pots of exotic flowering plants.

Everyone else in attendance had apparently understood what this type of gathering was about and how to dress for it—blazers for men, short dresses and high-heeled sandals for women—and what to bring or not bring. Fortunately, the big bowl of coleslaw she had arrived with had been discreetly whisked away by the maid that had answered the door when she arrived—and it didn't look like it would soon make an appearance on the long table loaded with elegant platters or on the trays held by the waiters that circulated through the crowd.

The guests weren't really eating much, anyway, she thought, because the food consumption she had witnessed could more accurately be described as "nibbling" or "tasting" or "sampling." Hot dogs, burgers, and chili—staples at the type of barbecue she was familiar with—were apparently not on the menu here, nor was ketchup. She doubted that ice cream and watermelon would make an appearance either.

Why had she even been invited, she wondered, and why had she accepted the invitation? Keeping to herself had been a longtime habit borne from a natural reserve that had only increased since moving East. She wasn't really shy or a hermit, but she generally preferred get-togethers with people you knew rather than large gatherings where you needed to be skilled at small talk and have a good supply of clever observations and amusing anecdotes.

Plus, she didn't work at something that anyone here would consider interesting. She was a children's librarian. Billina believed, *knew*, that librarians, contrary to popular mythology, were not really stern, and not really strict, and not really straitlaced. She knew that being a librarian required a sense of adventure, audacious curiosity, and a kind of intellectual gregariousness. She had those qualities, at least at work, but when it came to her social life, her personal life, she had to admit she was not someone who was comfortable around people like the people who seemed to have gathered here.

She recognized a few of the other guests and had picked up enough snippets of conversation to categorize them. There were some CEOs, financial analysts, people who did something or other with hedge funds, advertising maybe, people who represented companies, some who had been on television, a judge, a model, an athlete.

She admitted she was likely being unfair and painting with way too broad a brush. It was doubtless just a function of being in a new job, in a new town, in a new part of the country. Perhaps, she told herself, she should regard it as a learning experience rather than an ordeal.

Myra had been the one to ask her to come, but, Billina realized belatedly, it was probably sort of a mistake. Billina had walked out front to retrieve her newspaper and come upon Myra telling Zachary about the barbecue. She had probably felt obliged to invite Billina, too.

Billina had been renting the guest cottage behind Zachary Duncan's large rambling house since she had relocated from the Midwest. He had offered it to her because ... well, because he was nice, and he was on the library board, and when he heard the new Director of Children's Services was having trouble finding an affordable place in town, he had offered the cottage.

One kindness had led to more, and they had shared meals, and listened to music, and traded stories about where they grew up, and compared notes on favorite movies and baseball teams, and had become friends.

People sometimes didn't realize how hard it was to make friends once you were no longer in school, and not working in a big office, and not living in a small town where everyone knew everyone and had cousins who knew everyone else. Add to that the fact that she was well into her forties, and somehow still alone, and—what word could she use to describe herself? Unconventional? Eccentric? Either one would do, she supposed.

Reading stories to children, making them understand that magic, finding books, finding storytellers, singing songs, helping the older ones find the next book in whatever series they had fallen in love with—those were the things that she had always been passionate about—even well into her forties. And, she thought, with a trace of pride and a dose of defiance, she was damn good at her job. More than good. Her knowledge of children's literature was encyclopedic. She had taken graduate level courses in child development. She had served on a state panel examining the role of libraries in education and how to increase access to books. She had spoken on the topic of "book deserts" that affected communities in a similar way to "food deserts." She had spoken out about the harm of book bans.

Billina sighed. Such thoughts were for another day, another time, and another place. She snuck a glance at her watch. She had parked herself in a chair at the very edge of the patio hoping she wouldn't attract attention because of the way she was dressed. Before heading to the barbecue, she had donned a neat but very plain pair of blue jeans and a very ordinary top and a very practical pair of sneakers. She wondered how soon she could slip away from this very fashionable, very pretty, very glossy-magazine get-together.

"The acceptable leave-taking routine is to smile and wave goodbye to the hosts no earlier than fifty minutes after arriving. So you've got another, let's say, seventeen minutes to go." Zachary plopped into the chair next to her, grinning like the Cheshire Cat. He always grinned that way when he was pretty sure he had read her mind accurately. "But this is quite the stuffy gathering," he went on, "despite all the banter and laughter, so I don't think anyone will notice if we leave a little early."

"Why didn't you warn me about what to expect?" Billina asked, "and why did you come yourself if you knew it would be stuffy?"

"I came for exactly the same reason you came. It's nice to be nice to the neighbors, at least for fifty minutes."

"You might have given me a heads up about the dress code. You know I'm from the Midwest. We don't wear cocktail dresses and stilettos to backyard barbecues." She eyed his blazer.

"You have to forgive me," he said. "I should have mentioned that little detail. I've known Myra and Derek long enough to have figured out what sort of event this might be. I hope you'll overlook this small lapse and not fire me from my job and send me off without a letter of recommendation."

She laughed. "Remind me again. What exactly is your 'job' with respect to me?"

He grinned. "Isn't it obvious? I'm your official translator. I spent a few years in Chicago so I'm fluent in both Midwest and East Coast New England parlance. I also know several important dialects, like Fairfield County."

She giggled.

"I also consider it my duty to look after anyone who bears the honorable name of *Billina*."

She tilted her head to the side and gave him a speculative glance. "You've never brought up the topic of my name before. What do you know about the name Billina? I know you teach literature, but Billina isn't a name that appears in any of the books likely to appear on a college syllabus."

He drew himself up. "As a member of the library board, it's incumbent on me to know about all of our collections, not just the adult books. And, I'll have you know, my big sister read every single *Oz* book to me when I was a tyke. All fourteen of them. That's twice the number of the *Harry Potter* books, and, yes, I've read those, too."

"So you know about Billina. The Billina from the *Oz* books."

A big smile appeared on his face. "My sister, the way she read those books to me, it was one of the best things about my childhood. Mellie was almost ten years older than me. For my parents, I was what used to be called a late-in-life surprise. Probably not such a welcome surprise. But Mellie was delighted to have a sibling. She took care of me, spoiled me. When she read to me at bedtime, she did different voices for all the characters. I've seen you do story time at the library, and you do that, too. I'd always beg Mellie to read *one more chapter, pleeeease*, and usually she would. She did a great voice for Billina. Billina was important. Billina helped defeat the Nome King."

"By laying an egg."

"Yes. The Nome King eats it by accident and dies since eggs are poisonous to Nomes. All in all an excellent lesson for children on the power of female characters."

"At least the power of female chicken characters."

They looked at each other and started to laugh.

"My mother claims she didn't name me after that character," Billina said. "She claimed she combined the names Bill and Leena, which were her grandparents' names. I told her she should maybe have given the matter a little more thought and considered the possible detrimental effect on a child's self-esteem when she was teased on the schoolyard on account of her name."

"Were you teased on the schoolyard on account of your name?"

"Not too often. Not for long. There was a rather hurtful incident when Gregory Jones made clucking sounds when he saw me out on the playground, but I handled it, and it didn't happen again."

"How did you handle it?"

"I decked him."

Zachary threw back his head and laughed.

A reluctant smile appeared on Billina's face.

Zachary looked at his watch then rose to his feet. "We've made it through our obligatory fifty minutes. How about we go back home, have a couple burgers, and watch the game?"

"That sounds lovely," Billina said. "And let's stop by the kitchen on the way out. I can probably retrieve my coleslaw."

# At Lunch

Elsie

The restaurant had been Margo's choice. It had a French name. A long French name. Elsie couldn't remember what it was. Maybe she had suppressed the name after mispronouncing it when looking at the menu, eliciting an eyeroll and trill of laughter from her friend.

"Let me order, dear," Margo had insisted. "I know the chef, and he'll do something special for us."

Apparently she did, and he had because elegant luncheon entrees had been delivered in short order along with a cocktail for Margo. Elsie had said she'd stick with water—tap water, she specified, in answer to the waiter's query. But Margo had pulled her mouth into an expression of disapproval and told the waiter to bring a bottle of crystal artesian something-or-other to the table.

As Margo talked—well, talked and waved and traded mischievous side glances with some of the other patrons—Elsie took her fork and fiddled with the items on her plate. Before long, the chef's artfully arranged creation had been pushed into a small domed pile.

Elsie took stock of what was there. Three random tomatoes, each a different color, none of them red. A fig. A few stalks of cold asparagus sprinkled with sesame seeds. A slice of—what was that? Duck breast, she recalled. She recognized beets, watercress, arugula. She estimated the weight of the pile at something just over sixteen ounces. Given the price for the plate, plus drinks, plus tip, the price per pound hovered near the triple digit mark.

She picked up her fork again and ate one of the tomatoes. The purple one. It was a very good tomato, but she found herself calculating its cost. She was clever that way, able to do sums in her head while still offering a comment or two to punctuate Margo's soliloquy on whatever the *news* or *story* or *tittle tattle* happened to be at the moment. That was how Margo was clever—always knowing what was what. What was *of the moment*: the fashion, the rage, the trend, the story, the whim.

Elsie refocused on her food. An ounce, she decided. The tomato weighed about an ounce, so its monetary value to the restaurant was … yikes. That was one hell of an expensive tomato. Of course, not everything in the pile was of equal value, she reminded herself. The duck breast would have made up a larger portion of the price tag. Tomatoes, even heirloom tomatoes, would cost less.

She found herself thinking about Nanna. Nanna grew the best tomatoes in the whole county. Red ones. She had been intending to drive out to see Nanna, but Margo had cajoled her into postponing. She felt bad about that. Her weekly visits to her grandmother's house had started as an obligation—she was the only family member that still lived close by—but had become something she looked forward to. Sometimes she visited more than once a week. They worked in the garden together, or cooked, or played Scrabble. Nanna was a good painter and was giving her watercolor lessons. And they talked. About books, movies, jobs, where they had traveled, who they had loved, and who they loved still.

She probably should have found a way to sidestep this lunch, but Margo was not easily side-stepped.

"You know you want to come," Margo had coaxed. "You know you want to try …." Elsie still couldn't remember the name of this restaurant. "It's *the* place to be. To see and be seen."

With the tip of her knife, Elsie began to deconstruct the dome on her plate and rearrange the food. The remaining tomatoes became eyes. The fig, a giant nose. The duck was poked into the shape of a yawning mouth. Watercress and arugula became hanks of green hair. If she cut a beet in half, she'd have two red ears.

She hadn't been attending to Margo. The last words she had heard were "I needed a smaller size, of course …." But she noticed when Margo stopped talking and knew what came next.

It was time for Margo to make a scene, just a small one, loud enough to be heard, but not loud enough to make anyone think she was anything other than a very clever, very attractive woman having a bit of fun with a friend. Elsie, as the friend, would be the cause and butt of the commentary. The commentary would be scathing, but funny. Margo was gifted that way, always getting just the right balance between sarcasm and satire.

"Really, sweetie," Margo began, "Francois doesn't offer a discounted kiddie plate. And I don't think his recipes are meant to be *interactive*. We needn't make happy faces out of the food." She laughed. Laughed in the way someone does when she knows she has a good laugh, the kind of laugh that makes others laugh, too. The others would look at her with a kind of admiration. Someone that beautiful, someone that laughed that way, was someone exciting and important. Someone whose presence was worthy of comment.

Elsie laughed, too, and blushed. She understood that her role was to be just as entertained as everyone else who heard. Margo had always complimented her on her ability to laugh at herself.

"You're so good natured," she would coo. "It takes a special kind of person to be able to laugh at oneself. It takes modesty, I guess. And a big heart."

Elsie had always responded to that line about having a big heart, even though she suspected Margo of manipulation rather than admiration. She suspected Margo had little understanding of the dimensions of people's hearts and the complexities within them.

## Margo

Peeking out from beneath her eyelashes, Margo could see that the man at the next table had heard her comments, joined her laughter, reacted to the scene, and nudged his companion. It was fortuitous that they were seated nearby. One wrote for one of the New York magazines. The other was a prominent influencer. Maybe she would get a mention.

She saw that Elsie, too, was laughing, as she always did.

But then, the unexpected. Elsie dropped her napkin on the table, rose from her chair, and pushed it in.

Margo watched warily and thought about asking, "Where are you going?" But she felt wrong-footed. Her ability to riff, to spin sharp little observations, had been interrupted, and she suddenly felt like she had missed something. Like missing a cue on stage, a step in a dance, a thread in a conversation.

"I think I'm going to head out to Nanna's now," Elsie said. "She makes the best grilled cheese and tomato sandwiches, and maybe we can play a game of Scrabble. She'll probably beat me, but that's okay. She's good with words, you know. Not quite in the way you are, but still …."

Elsie picked up her handbag, fished out some bills, and placed them next to her plate. Then she leaned across the table and kissed Margo on the top of her head. "Goodbye, dear."

# High Rollers

He picked up the photo from the pile of papers in Gran's bottom dresser drawer, took a look at it, and laughed. The drawer was where Gran stored all the years of miscellany she felt was too precious to throw away and intended to sort: greeting cards from when people wrote greeting cards, faded notes from when people wrote notes, and wrote them in script, snapshots, a ribbon that maybe had adorned a corsage, ticket stubs from a ballgame or a play. He had offered to help her sort and organize the dresser drawer collection, a process that had taken a few weeks already. He was happy that he had. There had been some lovely surprises and wonderful stories to go along with them.

A friend had commended him for helping his great-grandmother with "death cleaning." He had felt a flash of anger. "It's not about that," he'd snapped. He'd almost launched into a retort, almost said more, then stopped. People would get it, or they wouldn't. If they'd never had the chance to know someone like Gran … their loss.

The photo he held was a black-and-white image showing three chorus girls, all brunettes. From the fifties maybe? The forties? Their arms circled each other's waists, their feet—clad in black tap shoes—were posed in a dance position as if they were ready to start a routine. Their smiles were outlined with the same bold lipstick, their heads sported the same shoulder-length curled hair. And the costumes!

He shook his head then walked to the kitchen where Gran sat at the table, the sun pouring in, the steam rising from the teacups.

"Gran, tell me about this." He handed the photo to the old woman, who took one look and laughed, then shook her head, tsked, and laughed again.

"The High Rollers," she said. "That's what the chorus girls were called. That's me on the right, Cath in the middle, and Babs on the left."

He studied the picture again. "Yes, okay, I can kinda see a resemblance between you and this dancer. You're prettier now, though."

She laughed again. "You're my favorite great-grandchild."

"You say that every time I'm here. You also say it to Sookie, and Ned, and Dawn, and Isaac, and—"

"It's not fair to point out that kind of inconsistency," she said in a reproving tone. "When you reach my age, things can get a little fuzzy and mixed up."

"Hah, right." He invested the words with ample sarcasm. "You can't pull that 'sweet little old lady' stuff on me. I'm onto you. But really, I want to know, tell me about the picture."

"It was when I lived in Las Vegas with my parents."

"I sorta figured, given that there are dice on the costumes."

"I applied for work in one of the hotels that had a big floor show. They weren't too fussy about age restrictions back then—not for the customers and not for the staff. I was considering my options from the jobs available, and I figured I could earn more dancing than I could cleaning rooms or waiting tables. I told my folks I was going to audition, and they were worried about me but said all right give it a try. My mamma talked to me about what men might try to do with a chorus girl. Course she knew men might try the same thing with someone making up a room. She also had my daddy teach me a couple ways to discourage unwanted advances. Daddy had been in the army, and done a little boxing, and been in some tight corners here and there, so he was a good one to teach me. So, when I got the job, I felt good and ready."

"How old were you?"

"Fifteen. I was tall for my age. Cath and Babs were twenty. They took me under their wing and looked out for me, and we became friends."

"What about school?"

"Well, I had finished up through the tenth grade, and we needed the money because it wasn't like now where you could get disability, and Daddy was getting up in years, and you know Mamma's eyesight wasn't any too good, so it made sense for me to work. I went back later and got my G.E.D. and started my college classes when things weren't quite so stretched thin."

"They had G.E.D. degrees back then, in the Jurassic period?"

"Very funny. The G.E.D. program was started during the war because so many young men were going into the military before they finished high school, and some of the girls were quitting school, too, to do wartime work in the factories."

"So you followed your dream onto the dance floor?"

"It wasn't really my dream to dance. Well, maybe a little. But not that kind of dancing. If I dreamt about dancing, I dreamt about Martha Graham and wearing a leotard and being in a room full of beatniks smoking cigarettes somewhere in New York City. I didn't think about wearing a costume with dice patterns sewn on. Did you notice that there's dice positioned right over our breasts—dice with the number one showing? Like it was their way to make us have nipples."

"On square breasts."

"Yep. Cath, Babs, and I all had the same reaction to the way the bodice looked. We had to avoid looking at each other or we'd start giggling. Why anyone considered such an outfit sexy, I'll never know."

"So dancing wasn't your dream?"

"I don't think I had a dream back then. I was just busy working the shows and getting used to the late hours. Or maybe I had a million dreams and just didn't have a lot of time to consider them more than a minute or two a day. I had dreams of finishing school and then maybe teaching school. I liked being with little kids. I wanted to marry a boy that would treat me nice like the way Daddy treated Mamma. Some days I wanted to live in New York City, like I said. Other days I wanted to live somewhere that had more flowers than neon lights. I didn't want to stay up late worrying about things. I wanted my own washing machine and dryer. I wanted to go to the library every week."

"What about your friends? Cath and Babs?"

"Cath, yes, her dream was the dancing. She was good, too. The best one of the three of us. She kept in the business and was even in a couple movies, not in any big parts with a lot of lines, you know. But in pictures that showed chorus girls or had big dance numbers."

"And Babs?"

"Babs wanted to settle down."

"And find a nice boy?"

"A nice girl. She was sorta hoping it would be Cath, but it wasn't. But it was okay because they stayed friends. And Babs eventually met Janet, and they fell in love."

"And lived happily ever after?"

"They did, oddly enough. Even though it was a hard time for two girls to be in love."

He eyed Gran for a moment. "I'm thinking about your million dreams. You got a lot of them, didn't you? The nice boy. The flowers. Teaching school."

"I did." She took a sip of tea then picked up the photo again. "You know, I think it's better to have a lot of dreams. Better than just one dream. Being adaptable and open means you can keep going. I still have dreams. Maybe not a million dreams. But a couple thousand."

"Gran, you *are* more beautiful now than you were in that picture."

"And you *are* my favorite great-grandchild. Well, you and—"

They laughed and recited together, "Sookie, and Ned, and Dawn, and Isaac, and …"

# Mix-Up

Lenore took a deep breath, all the way in, all the way out. Just as if she were in physical education class, walking up to the starting line of the fifty-yard dash. She had never won the fifty-yard dash. She wasn't a talented athlete like some of the girls. And she hated the one-piece green gym outfits that looked baggy—looked ugly—on almost everyone who donned one.

Her friend Karen had taken hers apart and done something with it—maybe put a few darts in the top and taken in a seam and hemmed the shorts—and it looked … better. But Lenore wasn't talented at sewing either. Or any of the other skills taught in home economics class. If it had been up to her, she would have skipped home economics class completely, but it was required for girls who wanted to graduate, so she had struggled through each of the units: sewing, cooking, childcare, and household financial management.

It was a good thing Karen had helped her with her final sewing project—an A-line skirt with a waistband and side zipper—because otherwise she would have failed, or maybe passed with a D which was almost as bad and would have ruined her grade point average. And she had returned the favor by letting Karen copy her answers on the household financial management test.

Financial management—now that was something she was good at. Better than good. All it really involved was math. Math for the housewife. Math for that day in the future when your husband would provide a weekly allowance so you could shop for groceries and cleaning products and maybe save up for something special like a dishwasher or a sewing machine.

*If fresh beef liver is thirty-five cents a pound, and you buy four and a half pounds and you get 20 percent off, how much will you spend?*

Karen had laughed at that question. "The real answer would be 'zero' because I hate liver. And I'd never marry a man who wanted me to serve him liver. I'd ask the butcher for steak."

Lenore had laughed, too, but reflected to herself that Karen was a girl from a family that could afford to eat steak every week—every day if they wanted to. Her father owned a company that made adding machines and cash registers, and they lived in a really nice house with a color television set in the living room and a Cadillac parked in the driveway.

Things were different in her own home. Her father worked in a garage, pumping gas and repairing cars. He made enough to feed his family—Lenore, her mom, her twin brother Leonard, and her little brother Scott—but steak wasn't often on the menu.

She knew that college wasn't likely to be on the menu either. Not for her. Not without a scholarship. Mom and Dad had sat with her at the kitchen table one night and explained it all. They couldn't afford to send both her and Leonard, especially with Scott coming along toward graduation in just a few years. And her brothers could go so much further if they became college boys—it would give them a chance, a future. Dad hadn't even finished high school, and he knew what that meant for a man. Plus, her parents pointed out, she had other options. She could take a secretarial course and learn typing and shorthand. Or maybe work as a hostess at the Empire Restaurant in town. It wouldn't be forever, only till she got married. Mom had taken her hand and squeezed it.

Lenore hadn't resented her parents for making this decision. She knew the world was just the world. And she was, after all, very good at household financial management and knew enough about her father's salary, the cost of groceries, mortgage payments, and how the taxes figured in to know that college for both her brothers and her was just not possible.

Not unless—here she took another one of those deep breaths—not unless she could earn a scholarship. Which was why she was sitting on a chair in the hallway outside the principal's office. When she had first arrived, there had been a dozen chairs, and a dozen students on those chairs, dressed in their best and waiting for their turn to be interviewed for a chance at a scholarship.

Garfield Township High School had, for many years, offered three scholarships to graduating seniors. There was the Valedictorian Award which went to the graduating senior with the highest grade point average, and two Excelsior Scholarships for the boy and girl who demonstrated excellence in a major field of study. Most of the boys who were candidates were planning to study engineering, although at times the award had been given to a young man who excelled in history or literature. The girls were most often those who planned to become schoolteachers or nurses, or those who had shown exceptional promise in home economics.

Lenore knew she would not be awarded any of these three scholarships. But this year, there was to be a fourth award. Mr. Hoffman, who had worked with British intelligence during the war before moving to the United States, had announced he was establishing a scholarship in mathematics. To apply, a student needed to write a letter explaining why he wanted to study this field and write an essay on a topic related to mathematics.

Mr. Abbott, the principal, had announced the new scholarship at the senior spring banquet. "The young man who is interested in applying for this award, will need to have completed all coursework within the mathematics department," he had said. "That will include algebra, geometry, and both trigonometry and calculus."

Mr. Abbott had spoken about the applicants as young men not because the scholarship was limited to boys, but because most of the students who had completed the required classes were boys. Most, Lenore thought, but not all.

Lenore knew it was her turn to interview when she heard Mr. Abbott's voice calling from inside his office. "Come on in, Leo, you're the last one."

Mr. Abbott was looking down at a stack of papers on his desk as she entered the room. Lenore could see that the paper on top was hers—the paper she had worked on for weeks. The paper that had taken every bit of free time she had. She had taken a risk by not writing about one of the traditional mathematics fields but had instead prepared a comprehensive explanation of the IBM 026 Printing Card Key Punch and the advantages gained by use of a Program Drum and how a Verifier could help avoid serious transcription errors.

Carefully, Lenore slid into a chair in front of the principal's desk. His eyes were still on her paper. He started speaking before looking up.

"Leonard, this essay is extraordinary. Very impressive indeed, but you have not taken calculus, and by the terms of the scholarship—"

It was then that he looked up. Looked up and saw her. Saw that she wasn't Leonard.

"Um, Miss Kaminsky, I'm afraid there's been a bit of a mix-up. We've completed the interviews for the Young Ladies' Excelsior scholarship. It's my understanding you did not apply for that award. And I was expecting your brother here to discuss his essay."

Lenore had to hold back from taking another deep breath. "That's not my brother's paper," she said. "It's mine."

"But it bears your brother's name, young lady." Mr. Abbott frowned and looked back down at the paper. "It says 'Leo Kaminsky.'"

"When we were little, we had nicknames," Lenore explained. She could feel her heart thumping in her chest. "His nickname is Lennie. Mine is Leo, like the lion. My brother always said I was like a lion when I got mad."

"Is there a reason you did not use your full given name on your essay?"

Lenore knew this was going to be the hardest question to answer. The question that a lot of men, a lot of people, just didn't understand. "I thought …," this time she didn't hold back on taking a big breath, "I thought you might not read it if you knew it was written by a girl. Or might not read it in the same way."

Lenore could tell Mr. Abbott did not quite know how to respond to this—whether to be angry or amused or offended or officious. She understood. When the idea had first occurred to her, she had cycled through emotions herself. First there was the satisfaction of finding a solution to the doubt that had been nagging at her—doubt that she would receive a fair hearing. Then there was anger because such a deception was necessary. Then the shame appeared. She had ended up with resolve and defiance.

"I've taken calculus, Mr. Abbott. And trig. I was top in the class in trig."

"Were you top in calculus as well?" Mr. Abbott looked like he was going in the direction of amusement.

"I tied with Keith Reynolds. But he didn't apply because he's going to be working with his dad at the dairy. But I don't think that matters. I think what matters is what I've figured out about improvements in computer programming that could be made with changes to the technology, and what might be possible in the future with the development of miniaturization. Would you like me to take you through that?"

She waited. It wasn't clear what Mr. Abbott was thinking. He wrinkled his brow and looked down at her paper then back up at her. Finally—she could see this with her own eyes—he took a deep breath, just like he was standing at the starting line of the fifty-yard dash and gave her a nod.

She smiled and began.

# Zinnias

I try to keep my mind on the gardening. I pull three dandelions, not because I dislike dandelions, I'm not that kind of person, but because I want the new little flowers I brought to have room to stretch and grow.

Zinnias are a good choice. I got a lot of different colors from the seeds I collected last year. I think zinnias look best when the colors are all mixed up together. It makes it look like a friendly group of people, all with different colored faces: pink, purple, yellow, orange.

Another thing I like about them is that they grow tall. In Momma's garden they'd be knee high, even waist high. She was something special when it came to gardening.

I need to keep my mind on what I'm doing. I take each little flower from the container I had put it in. I had started them all up on my windowsill when it was still cold outside. I didn't really have little garden pots, so I'd used paper cups, like the ones you get at Dunkin' Donuts when you order coffee. If I went through the drive-through before work, I'd save the cup, and rinse it out at home, and put a little soil in it and some of the flower seeds. Sometimes, I'd trim down an empty milk carton and use that, too.

I'm happy it's Saturday, so I have time for this. It's beautiful outside. The sky's as blue as that pretty dress Momma used to wear. It was blue-and-white checked, and she said it made her look too young, like Dorothy Gale in *The Wizard of Oz*, but it didn't at all. It had a round neckline and a white lacy kind of collar, and a full skirt. She wore that dress when she and Daddy went out dancing.

I sit back on my heels and think about how to put in the zinnias. I don't think I want them in rows. I think I want them scattered here and there and everywhere. I want them to be unorganized, a little wild. Carefree. That's what I want.

Rows make me think about soldiers. Or lines of print in a newspaper. I don't want to think about the newspaper I read yesterday evening. I don't want to think about the lady killed by her boyfriend. Thinking about that makes me think about the reason it might have happened. Every day, Monday through Friday, when I'm on the other end of the women's center hotline, I hear the reasons. The women tell me the reasons. A lot of times they tell me the reasons like they're talking in the voice of the man that screamed at them or hit them or cut them or waved a gun in their face.

*Because she talked back.*
*Because dinner was cold.*
*Because she complained.*
*Because she was ugly.*
*Because I wanted another drink.*
*Because of the money.*
*Because the house wasn't clean.*
*Because she flirted with that guy at the bar.*
*Because she wouldn't shut up.*
*Because she deserved it.*
*Because I had a hard day.*
*Because the kid was fussing while the game was on.*
*Because she had to learn who's boss.*
*Because she asked where I was last night.*
*Because I felt like it.*

I think I've heard a hundred of these reasons, maybe a thousand. All different and all the same. Except sometimes, sometimes there's that one-in-a-thousand voice that cuts through a lot of bullshit. That voice says, "The reason is because I like having the power to hurt."

I don't want to think about those voices. It's Saturday. The sky is blue. I'm planting flowers. The voice I'll hear is Momma's voice. She told it to me straight.

"Daddy and I both came from homes with a lot of fights. His Pappy once hit him and knocked him over the kitchen table. My father drank, and we were all scared of him. It was the Depression. We didn't have anything. Maybe that's the reason, but it's not a reason that's good enough. So, when Daddy and I married we vowed in the church to love and honor. But we made another vow, just us two, before we ever set foot in that church. It was just as solemn, just as much in front of God.

No yelling. No hitting. Not ever. Not for any reason. Your Daddy and I aren't perfect, not by a long shot, but we kept that vow."

I better hurry up and finish with these flowers. Momma's grave is going to look grand. I've divided the flowers, so I can put the same ones on Daddy's grave. They're buried right next to each other. It's like a symbol, saying something about how they always stayed in love and were kind to each other, seeming almost like they've just come home from dancing and are sleeping right close with flowers all around.

Another thing about zinnias. If you pick one, another will grow on the same stem. Sometimes two will grow. And if you cut those, more will come. One kind of zinnia is called "Cut and Come Again" because of that quality.

That's what people need, sometimes. The ability, after being cut down and cut back, to rise up all over again. More. Better. Better than ever.

# Lifestyle

It would be a quick way to make money. That was the bottom line, and that was why Wendy had asked for a whole month off. A month of temp work doing set-up for the rich lady's tag sale easily outdistanced a month at Shorty's. Actually, it outdistanced three months at Shorty's where she took orders, placed plates before truckers at the counter, and served families out for a meal at the end of the week sitting in one of the booths. Eggs, home fries, bacon or sausage in the morning. Sometimes pancakes. Shorty made great pancakes, and the whole town knew it. They were served with real maple syrup, not that fake stuff. The rest of the day and into the evening it was burgers and fries or BLTs or grilled chicken. Every now and then a vegetarian or old hippie would wander in, and she'd direct him, her, or them to the list of salads. Shorty did fine with salads, too. He had a reputation to uphold, after all, and a satisfied customer would come back again, and maybe would come back over and over again and be a regular.

Shorty had understood why she wanted a month off to snag that extra pay. He knew she had started classes at the community college, and the money would come in handy. The rich lady offering the big money for work at her *made-for-TV*, supposedly *all-for-charity* tag sale was that TV show host, homemaker guru, women's magazine darling, runway "radiant presence," front-page tabloid celebrity—from back when people actually picked up tabloids at their grocery stores—and, most importantly, in her latest iteration, *lifestyle authority*.

She was referred to simply as "the rich lady" by everyone in the county, everyone Wendy knew, people living normal lives, because, when you got right down to it, that was what she was. True, other wealthy locals weren't given that kind of title, but they'd all been around long enough so that people knew who they were and what they were really like. Mrs. Farrington, who had donated to the hospital and the local library, was just Mrs. Farrington or sometimes "Old Lady Farrington." Judge McGraw was just Judge McGraw, or "Your Honor," or Kevin if you were one of the people—and there were plenty still around—who had seen him lead the basketball team to a state championship way back in the day.

But when the rich lady had arrived a few years back, purchasing a big piece of land about five miles outside of town and constructing a sprawling estate, she was already carrying a load of identities too numerous to keep track of. There were the characters she had played, the nicknames coined in the press, the names associated with her TV shows, the titles given her by the designers she represented. It was all too complicated if you had work to get to, groceries to purchase, meals to make, kids to take care of, and bills to pay. Who had time to follow all that other stuff?

The ad that had lured Wendy from Shorty's had gone up in early June. It offered one month of employment at the rich lady's estate. Workers were needed to help prepare for the tag sale, needed to set up tents, unpack objects from storage, carry items outside, and arrange displays. On the day of the sale, workers would be needed to answer questions, serve customers, and load purchases, all while looking helpful and happy and respectful in an all-American but still Downton Abbey sort of way. Tickets to get into the sale cost north of a hundred dollars, and it was going to be filmed and broadcast on television. So there was that, too. The chance to appear on the screen, maybe exchange a few clever quips with a celebrity customer or the rich lady herself, was a unique opportunity.

Wendy hadn't cared about that part of the deal. It was the pay that mattered. It was far more than was usually available for those, like her, who only had a high school diploma, and had just started her journey along the road to a college education, one course at a time.

She had explained it all to Shorty late one night after her shift was done. He had understood and agreed and promised to hold her job for her. She knew he would keep his promise in the same way she knew the sun rose in the east. And he had. Shorty was that kind of man, and Shorty's was that kind of place.

Shorty's was open till ten every night except Sunday. She worked the late shift most nights because it was easier for her than the gals that had families at home, kids. She didn't mind the clean-up chores. There was a relaxed kind of camaraderie when the outside lights were shut off, and it was just her and Shorty and Donny.

Shorty did most of the kitchen clean-up because Shorty liked to keep his own kingdom in order. He said his dad had taught him that, and it was good advice. Donny, who claimed to have been a wrestler in his youth, would help out in the kitchen and also do what he called the "he-man" jobs of carrying out the trash, mopping the floors, and washing down the counters.

Donny did the Ladies' and Gents' rooms, too. Well, actually, the bathrooms were now officially unisex. The customers hadn't seemed to mind when the signs were changed. Wendy thought it was because Shorty had commissioned new signs from one of the old hippie regulars who was a really good artist and had done some nice murals on a few of the older buildings in town. The doors now said, "Restroom for Who-ever" and there were little Dr. Seuss-type Whoville characters on the signs with funny hairstyles and clothing, and it was kind of a joke because it was more grammatically correct to say "Whomever," but the characters made everyone laugh, and no one seemed to be worried about—God forbid—somebody with a different identity using the bathroom.

The clean-up jobs that Wendy handled were categorized in her mind, and she ticked them off as they were completed. Loading and unloading the dishwasher. Laundering towels, aprons, uniforms, and linens. Container-filling: ketchup, sugar, salt, and pepper. Then straightening. Straightening could be, and usually was, a whole variety of things. Making sure the menus were neatly stacked and wiped free of stains. Making sure the bins for dishes and trays for the servers were properly arranged. Putting notices on the small bulletin board at the entrance—like a newspaper picture of the kids who made honor roll, or a photo of an oldster celebrating 100 years with a birthday cake and champagne. Finally, making sure the vases that held the flowers were cleared of fading blossoms, rinsed, and ready for the morning.

Wendy had been the one to suggest the fresh flowers.

"Your dad's garden is full of beautiful flowers," she had pointed out. "Having fresh flowers on the table is like having real maple syrup. It's nice. It's real. It makes Shorty's special."

Shorty had agreed, and now fresh flowers were put out every morning.

Shorty wasn't his real name, of course. It was Tom. Shorty was a nickname, and it hadn't been given to him because he was short. He was six foot three, with broad shoulders, really nice black hair, brown eyes, and ears that stuck out a little bit. He was only called Shorty because he was a short order cook, and it was kind of a joke that made people laugh. Sort of like the signs on the bathroom doors. A good kind of laughing.

As she worked, Wendy reflected back on the month she had been gone, the month spent at the rich lady's estate. It had, indeed, been a quick way to make money. The work was exactly as described, and she had done it well. She had been assigned to setting up displays after one of the many supervisors had seen and approved of her rather nice efforts at arranging sets of china and glassware. Plus, her skinny build had, apparently, made her a poor choice for carrying crates and loading up trucks. Wendy had thought briefly of Donny and his laughing reference to the "he-man" jobs.

So, Wendy had set up displays. After the china and glassware, there were linens, cutlery, silverware, figurines, teapots, bowls, and flower vases. She had especially loved the vases, many of them antique. Her suggestion of adding fresh flowers to a few of the more stunning examples was well received and acted upon. The flowers added were not the marigolds and zinnias used at Shorty's. Peonies, roses, hydrangeas, and lilies in the loveliest shades were delivered on the day of the sale, and carefully arranged by a florist that came in from New York.

The sale itself had been a whirlwind, sort of like a day at Shorty's after a football game or on the eve of a holiday. Except for a few key differences. Like the television cameras that seemed to be everywhere. Wendy had caught a few glimpses of her employer surrounded by aides and people who fussed with her hair or make-up. She had also seen and recognized some of the well-known "personalities" who had made an appearance.

In the tent where Wendy was assigned to work, the nicely dressed customers asked questions about the history of this piece or that, the provenance of a vase or sugar bowl. Some of them posed for pictures near the signs, posted everywhere, that had images of the rich lady smiling, and the message "Luminous Lifestyle" which apparently was the PR team's branding slogan for the event.

Yes, it had been a quick way to make money, Wendy thought, and interesting in a certain kind of way. But now here she was at Shorty's again, closing up after her first day back. The bathroom doors had been propped open, and she could hear Donny singing off-key. He had smiled broadly to welcome her return, and now was doing a robust version of "How you gonna keep 'em down on the farm, after they've seen Paree …."

She was almost finished with her straightening chores. She popped into the kitchen and saw that Shorty was nearly done as well. He grinned when he saw her.

"How was your return to Earth after your visit to the stars? To Never Never Land, the Land of Oz. I hope …," he raised an eyebrow and searched her face, hesitating, "I hope we don't seem too ordinary."

For a minute Wendy thought about a beautiful pink vase at the tag sale. It had been filled with roses and priced at well over five hundred dollars. Her plans for the following day at Shorty's included daisies for the vases at the tables and booths. Daisies were in bloom in her garden. She looked around the spotless kitchen then studied his face. It was a handsome face, she thought, even those ears that stuck out a little bit.

"Everything there was beautiful, but …." Now she was the one looking for words. Then she knew the right ones, knew in the same way she knew the sun rose in the east. "I'm glad to be back," she said. "There's no place like here. There's no place like home."

# Suitable Female Occupation, 1905

Abigail Gilborne sat at the edge of a chair in her father's office, located on the third floor of Gilborne's Emporium. Both of her parents were present, her father behind his desk and her mother standing sentry by the shelf that held the pattern books, order forms, catalogues, and accounting records. Abigail recognized this meeting as the culmination of a series of similar meetings that had been held fairly often in her seventeen years of life, at least once she had set aside her pinafore and donned long skirts.

Abigail knew that her parents believed the question to be addressed was this: What employment within the Emporium would be suitable for their youngest child—an awkward, homely child—now that she had completed school? Abigail hoped she had the courage to provide the answer she had arrived at after serious reflection. The answer was this: No employment within the Emporium would suit her. None at all.

In her mind, she rehearsed the argument to be made, going over each point in order, in the same way she did when practicing for a school recitation or debate.

*Introduction to Argument and Thesis Statement: I am not well-fitted for work in the Emporium. I would do far better, and be happier, employed elsewhere.*

The Emporium, her father's "empire," was housed in a fine building that stretched the length of the block. Well-to-do women flocked to the Emporium with the expectation of excellent service from attentive clerks and a remarkable offering of fine fashions—morning dresses, skirts and waists, ballgowns, hats, gloves, jewelry, corsets and other pretty undergarments. While the Emporium was not as large as Macy's in New York City or Marshall Field's in Chicago, it was modeled after them, adhered to the same high standards, and attracted the same class of customers.

*Argument Point One: I am different from other members of my family.*

Abigail knew that Papa's success was due in no small measure to his choice of a wife. Mama was attractive, had a good head for business, was excellent at maintaining important social connections, and used sense and firm discipline to manage the staff. Abigail's older siblings shared these qualities and had, each in turn, effected a seamless transition into the family business. Walter had taken over managing the accounts. Robert worked with Papa and the buyers who traveled the continent, and even sailed to Europe to obtain the finest quality merchandise. Even Evelyn had spent time in the store as a fashion consultant before her marriage to young Mr. Appleton, one of Papa's assistants.

Abigail knew that she was a puzzlement to her parents. It wasn't simply that she had been born when her mother was past forty. It was that she was born into a different world. Yes, her sister had attended school, but more as a way to acquire friendships and polish than as a serious academic endeavor. When Abigail began high school, more than a decade later, the girls did everything the boys did. They competed for academic honors, enrolled in the advanced mathematics and science classes, joined the debate team, and donned bloomers to play sports.

*Argument Point Two: My friends are embarking on exciting careers. I wish to do the same.*

Abigail wondered if she could explain this to her parents. For them, the Emporium was exciting, a magical palace, a bustling hub of luxury, entertainment, and enterprise. But Abigail had never regarded it that way. What intrigued and fascinated her, what set her mind racing with longing and anticipation, was spun from the animated discussions she had with her classmates about their plans for the future. Chloe and Anne were going to university. Eileen was already writing articles for one of the new magazines, *McClure's*, in New York City. Maribel would be traveling to Chicago to work with Jane Addams at Hull House. And Jonathan—her heart always gave a little skip when she thought about Jonathan—he would be reading the law with his father, Mr. Lloyd. After several years of apprenticeship, he would be prepared to take the bar exam.

*Argument Point Three: I do not have the right appearance for work at the Emporium.*

Abigail thought about the young women employed as salesclerks. They were expected to dress carefully, wear their hair in a neat but fashionable style, and care for their complexions. Their appearance was key to their success. If a gentleman was searching for a necklace for a lady friend, or a woman was seeking the perfect dress, it was important for the salesclerk to have a pretty smile, perhaps hold the necklace or the dress up to herself, and let the customer imagine that beauty in their own life.

Abigail could not imagine such a role for herself. When she was ten, she had overheard her mother telling her father about interviewing salesgirls for work in the millinery department. "I only hired two," she had reported. "I couldn't take on the Irish girl. Her look was right, but her accent was far too pronounced. It wouldn't have set the right tone. And then there was another young lady who spoke beautifully, but who …."

"Who what?" her father had asked.

"Who had a face like a horse," her mother admitted. She laughed ruefully. "It will be the problem we will need to address with Abigail."

Later, in her room, Abigail had pondered this bit of information as she examined her appearance in the standing mirror. Did she really look like a horse? She studied her face, ticking off her features. Maybe her nose was too long. Maybe, too, her jawline. She regarded her hair. Was her straight brown hair like a horse's mane? Her mother was fair-haired, and Evelyn's hair was a mass of chestnut curls. Abigail bared her teeth and thought about whether the horsey image was thereby enhanced. Perhaps it was, she thought. She didn't have Evelyn's even teeth and lovely smile.

*Argument Point Four: Mr. Lloyd has agreed to let me read the law and apprentice, along with Jonathan. He will take us both into his office.*

Jonathan had asked on her behalf, and Mr. Lloyd had readily agreed. He was a prominent member of the community and well-known for the progressive causes he supported. His office was busy, and he needed assistance. He had not balked because she was female. His wife was a suffragist, and they both supported equality for women, scoffing at those who warned of the danger of "petticoat rule."

The Lloyds understood the friendship between Abigail and their son, although many others did not. Abigail and Jonathan were the finest scholars in the class, always vying for firsts on examinations. And their competition did not prevent their mutual support. Abigail had helped

Jonathan with grammar and rhetoric. He had helped her with mathematics.

*Argument Point Five ....*

Abigail wasn't exactly sure how to express Point Five. It had something to do with a conversation she had had with Jonathan on a sunny afternoon near the end of term as they sat on a park bench near a patch of daffodils.

"Listen," she had said, "here are my choices if I stay at the Emporium given that I can't sell and don't belong on the floor. I could type correspondence or prepare the displays or help with the books, but—"

"But accounting requires mathematics, and you don't care for mathematics," Johnathan pointed out. "You can accomplish it, but I suspect it is not how you wish to spend your time."

"And my brother handles the books and would not thank me for my interference." She thought a minute then shook her head. "What an odd thing to think about, to ponder."

"What?" he asked. "Mathematics?"

"No. To think about how I wish to spend my time. None of my siblings have reflected on such a thing. My brothers went to work in the Emporium. Evelyn too, before her marriage. The Emporium has been everything, the choice that is expected."

"Have you considered marriage?"

She gave him a look. "Marriage needn't supplant other occupation. Your own mother gives evidence of that. And, in any case, I have been given to understand that gentlemen desire something more from the young ladies they propose to."

"And what is that 'something more'?" he asked.

"They desire a wife that doesn't look like a horse," she stated.

He had thrown his head back and laughed, then, seeing the color rising in her cheeks, had taken hold of her hand. "For an intelligent woman, you ought to know better than to talk stupidly," he said. "And, I must tell you that not all men see things in the same way, do not all value others in the same way, may not see faces in the same manner."

When she didn't respond, he had raised an eyebrow. "You are usually ready with an answer, Abby. Cat got your tongue?"

The childish taunt had made her laugh. And then he had kissed her. No one had ever kissed her before.

After the kiss, he had kept hold of her hand. She noticed he was blushing. She noticed her friend—the brash, handsome boy who had always been her friend—was nervous, and hopeful, and waiting for her decision. First, she had smiled. Then she had kissed him back.

*Perhaps, it might be best not to mention Point Five to her parents.*

*Argument Conclusion: After careful consideration I have arrived at the understanding that I wish to spend my time preparing for a different future. That future will be in a different place and with different companions.*

Papa's voice interrupted her thoughts and brought her back to the moment, to the meeting.

"You wanted to talk to us, Abby?"

She nodded her head. She knew she was ready. "Yes, Papa, Mama. I have several things I wish to say."

# Miggs

The hallways at Benjamin Cardozo High School were deserted and dark, with only the emergency exit lights aglow. They provided just enough illumination for Miggs to walk up and down the corridors, pushing his custodian's cart and checking that all the classroom doors were locked.

It was Friday night, close to midnight, and even the most industrious teachers—the old workhorses that stayed late grading papers, or copying, or putting something up on one of the bulletin boards—had left for home hours ago. He had signed up for overtime hours, like he often did when a custodian was needed for an afterschool or evening event: a concert or play in the auditorium, a basketball game in the gym, or a meeting of the debate team or the chess club. Tonight it had been the annual chili cook-off.

The winner had been Tanya whose entry would be dubbed in next week's school paper as "the friendliest chili." Tanya had cemented that description by insisting, in her acceptance speech, that there really shouldn't be a "winner" and the cook-off shouldn't really be a "contest" because everyone that was there was there to have a good time, and people had different preferences when it came to chili, and maybe next year it should simply be a nice way to gather and eat chili and discuss recipes and build community. *Tanya was just that kind of kid,* he thought with a smile.

He completed his tour of the building ending up at the janitor's office next to the gym. He had been the one who had made it an office. In the past, it was just a storeroom where cleaning supplies were kept, along with buckets and mops. It was where the previous head custodian had installed a small portable TV on top of an old filing cabinet, and where the one before had put a radio that he kept tuned to the ball game.

Miggs had brought in an extra student desk, and a small bookshelf. He had asked the computer teacher for one of the school's laptops, explaining that keeping a building clean and in good order required more than the buckets and mops he had inherited from the previous head custodians.

There was a lot of interest now in "green cleaners," he explained. A lot that could be learned about ventilation and fire safety. The new principal, Mrs. Marie D'Angelo had agreed. So now he had an office. The school was lucky, he thought, to have Marie. She had taught math and science before earning a master's degree in administration and becoming a principal. She was clearly brilliant, and tough as nails, but she was … it had taken him a while to figure out the right word … *wise*. She knew when to listen and when to lay down the law. When to be the boss and when to be a motherly person who could give ear with patience and a box of tissues close at hand when a single mom, or a tough teen, or an overstressed teacher poured out their woes.

Mrs. D'Angelo had, at his insistence, ended the practice, common in past years, of assigning students serving detention to work with the custodians to do tasks such as scrubbing out the bathrooms. He had done a memo on that the very first week after her appointment and hand delivered it to her as she was still moving into her office.

"It's degrading," he explained, after she read the short, three-paragraph explanation he had typed out. "I'm not talking here about the regular way people think about it, that it's degrading to the students. Sure, there's that, but it's degrading to my staff, as well. It's saying our work is disgusting, and those of us who do it are sort of disgusting, too. And you would only do it as a punishment or as a last resort. It's like saying, 'if you don't shape up, you'll end up cleaning toilets.' It's like saying those of us who do this work are failures. It's not fair, and it's not accurate, and it's not right."

She had looked at him, looked down at the memo, looked at him again, and nodded. "You're right. I didn't realize that kind of thing was still being done. It won't happen from now on. Ever."

He had nodded his thanks, and turned to go, then stopped. "It's not that I mind working with the students. It's not that at all. Sometimes a kid just needs …," he paused because he wasn't sure what he wanted to say. A kid just needs what? Someone to listen who isn't a teacher? Someone that was more like a grandpa? Or needed a task that let you move around and use your hands? A chance to be creative with tools other than a pencil and paper?

Mrs. D'Angelo seemed to understand even though he couldn't complete the sentence. She nodded again. "You just let me know what you might have in mind, Mr. Miggs," she said.

And he had. Not often, but from time to time. He had asked one student who had been caught spraying graffiti on the dumpster outside to help him repaint his office. "You pick the colors," he had told the kid. "Something that will be easy to keep clean, but something that's, you know, cheerful and calming, too."

He had another kid sit at the laptop in his office and do a memo on mold in school buildings. The union had used the research in the memo to convince the administration that just replacing a discolored ceiling tile was insufficient and ineffective when it came to stopping the spread of this contaminant.

Another student, one who the old principal had labeled a troublemaker, a 'smart alec,' had been recruited to craft a wooden plaque that was now installed in the lobby next to the portrait of Benjamin Cardozo himself.

"Cardozo was a pretty good guy," the kid had told him as he applied a final coat of varnish to the plaque. "He was one of the 'three Musketeers' on the Supreme Court. They were the ones who supported Roosevelt's New Deal."

The old man had raised his eyebrows, and the kid looked a little embarrassed. "I'm not, you know, stupid," he said. "And I like Dr. Field's history class."

Miggs sighed, looked around his office—nicely painted in sage green with navy trim—to make sure everything was in its place, then turned off the lights and locked up. He headed down the hall to the one room that still had a light on and peeked in the door.

Ms. Peterson was perched on a stool at the counter, a fat cookbook open before her. As he expected, the Home Economics room was already washed, scrubbed, and neat as a pin. She heard him and looked up, grinning a welcome. "Well, another Benjamin Cardozo High School chili cook-off is in the record books," she said with a smile.

"If Tanya has her way, next year it won't be a cook-off. It will be the Benjamin Cardozo High School Community Chili Love-In."

"You know, that's not such a bad idea," she said. "I may side with Tanya on this one. I bet Marie would, too."

"Every kid gets a trophy?"

"Yes. When you're dealing with kids—these kids, our kids—every kid *deserves* a trophy. Especially when it comes to food."

He studied his friend with affection—her gray hair was pulled back in a ponytail. The apron she had donned for the cook-off looked like it should be popped in the washing machine. She looked a little tired, but not tired in a bad way. Only in the way an older person looked at the end of a long, but productive and satisfying day.

"I know we planned to get a late-night snack," he said, "but I'm afraid even the diner might be close to closing by now. I'm sorry it took so long to clean up."

"That's okay," she said. "Why don't I just make us some coffee here? And would you like a bowl of chili? I'm pretty sure I could find us some chili."

# Bertie Franklin Wynesco

Bertie Franklin Wynesco, Esquire, well-known ambulance chaser, snake-oil salesman, and con-man, knew he had stumbled onto a good thing that June afternoon among the dahlias and the daisies when he became the accidental eyewitness to an amorous encounter between Dalton Dence, the strait-laced, family-values, county council candidate and Sally Serenity Standish, former Woodrow Wilson High School prom queen and recent ex-girlfriend of Racetrack Ricky, Dogwood Flats' most notorious citizen.

Dence—"It's spelled with a C," he reminded the press—was riding high in the polls thanks to his rugged good looks, reputed moral rectitude, and compelling campaign catchphrases. More than one elector had been heard parroting his trademark slogans: *We need Piety in Society* and *Woke is a Joke*.

Ricky, on the other hand, was the CEO of a far-flung felonious enterprise encompassing a wide range of illicit endeavors. Ricky was known for fixing fights, nicking the odd truckload of electronics, selling knock-off designer handbags, extorting protection payments from pubs, and, on at least one occasion, demanding a cut of the profits from the senior citizens' Bull Moose Lodge barbecue and bingo game held every other Friday night from the Fourth of July through Labor Day.

Bertie, it must be said, had something of a reputation himself having converted three unremarkable years in law school and his inexplicable passing of the bar exam into a lucrative career. By regaling juries with sob stories of the grievous harm and crippling emotional distress suffered by his clients in fender benders that hardly justified a call to AAA, Bertie could convert the most frivolous lawsuit into a tidy profit for the plaintiffs, even after deducting one-third of the proceeds for his own well-deserved contingency fee.

This personal history had shaped Bertie's world view in not-so-subtle ways. He did not subscribe to the axiom that you can't make a silk purse out of a sow's ear. With courtroom cunning and eloquent oratory, he had made that particular transformation over and over again. Bertie *lived* for sows' ears. Sows' ears were his stock-in-trade.

But now, for the first time in his somewhat checkered career, Bertie found himself possessing a piece of knowledge that sparkled as brightly as a three-carat diamond on the finger of a TV-show bachelorette. If handled deftly, the titillating tryst, the clandestine conjugation—Bertie had yet to determine the final phraseology—between the blonde and buxom Sally Serenity and the right-wing poster boy might produce a stream of plenteousness he could sail to the land of milk and honey. Granted, blackmail was a little outside his usual playbook, but still, when opportunity knocks it behooves you to get off your ass and answer the door. And if Providence smiles, why not flash your pearly whites and enjoy the moment?

Bertie pondered the game ahead. The best result would see Dence behind the eight ball and Bertie himself in the cat bird seat. The suggestion that Dogwood Flats' most prominent pontificating prig had been covertly canoodling with a girl like Sally Serenity would be more than sufficient to topple his crusade like a house of cards.

Not that Sally Serenity was disliked. Not at all. What was disliked, what would cause Dence's campaign to go belly up, was the hypocrisy of the man.

Sally Serenity was already known fondly and accepted as a gal who liked a good time. She had never tried to hide the fact. She also laughed often, always donated to the United Way, bought raffle tickets and Girl Scout cookies from every kid that came to her door, and spoke her mind. If, every now and then, she stayed late at a local saloon and had "a few too many," she called herself a cab, sat in the back seat, rolled down the window if the weather was fine, and entertained the driver and all within earshot by glad-warbling all the way home.

Yes, there had been that relationship with Ricky, but she had ended it after the attempted extortion of the Bull Moose Lodge bingo game.

"My grandpappy and his friends love that game," she had explained to Ricky and a fair number of interested eavesdroppers, Bertie included, at the Dogwood Diner late one Friday night when everyone had migrated from the sports bar after a ninth-inning homer resulted in a loss for the Phillies, and the idea of eggs over easy and hash browns had pulled the whole crowd into the diner's booths. As the town's only twenty-four-hour establishment, it was the place to see, be seen, and gossip when every other hangout had shut off its lights and locked the door.

"It's one thing to tell some bimbo she's getting a genuine Yves Saint Laurent handbag for fifty-five dollars, *cash, no credit,*" Sally continued. "Anyone with any sense would know she's buying a pig in a poke. But there's no reason to mess with the bingo game, Ricky. You should know better than that."

The other patrons of the diner had nodded in silent agreement, and Ricky, always a man to know when the jig was up, had sheepishly agreed to never again interfere with any of the Bull Moose events, a list of which was published bi-weekly in their Lodge newsletter's calendar of activities.

The upshot of this conversation was a break-up of the relationship between Sally and Ricky which was, all in all, fairly amicable. Sally was never one to hold a grudge, but Ricky knew her ardor had cooled after his bingo game misstep. And, in any event, it wasn't as if either of them had been interested in taking a stroll down the aisle. They had parted on excellent terms with no hard feelings.

As he reflected on these events, several things occurred to Bertie. First, he suspected that the encounter he had witnessed in the flower fields was a one-off. Sally Serenity wasn't above satisfying her … curiosity, but didn't suffer fools gladly and would likely have no truck with that conservative clown long-term.

Second, once Bertie had convinced Dence to withdraw from the campaign to "spend more time with his family," a spot would open up for a candidate with a more liberal, more inclusive program. Bertie had always supported women in leadership positions. They made marvelous judges and even better jurors, and he, for one, had always believed Sally Serenity was destined for a position more important than prom queen. As for himself, he knew he'd make a dynamite campaign manager.

A brochure printed on Sunday-magazine shiny paper appeared in his mind: *Isn't it time for someone in county government who has a bigger vision, a bigger heart, and bigger breasts?* Pondering this, Bertie edited the slogan to eliminate the last of these defining qualifications. It made sense to him but might be taken amiss by elements of the electorate and Sally herself.

Standing in front of the mirror on the morning of his visit to Dence's office in the County Constituency, Bertie studied his appearance. Perhaps the stripes on his suit were a little too wide, the shine on his shoes a little too glossy, but when the world's your oyster, what's wrong with being a pearl? Outside the door, he paused by the garden to pick a perfect pink rosebud and place it in his lapel. It was going to be a beautiful day.

# Crossing the Desert, 1958

We got up early to cross the desert. Way early. Before the sun came up. The only way to cross a long stretch of Nevada desert and make it bearable is to race west in predawn coolness, rolling down the windows to catch the rush of wind, eating up miles in the darkness.

Now look, if you take on Apollo with a Ford Country Squire station wagon, Apollo's going to win every single time. But we'd get in a hundred miles, a hundred-fifty miles, before the ball-of-fire chariot rose over the distant mountains, shot its arrow of light into our rear-view mirror, and set the sand and the air itself on broil.

When it's 1958 there's no car air conditioning. No seat belts. No speed limits. No limits on adventure once the magic month of August arrives. Dad gets two weeks of vacation, so we pile suitcases into the car, pile ourselves into the car—Mom, Dad, the four of us kids—and set off.

Our starting point is Wilmette, just north of Chicago. Our destination is Grandma and Pops' place in Los Angeles, California. The route will be a grand loop through the West. Heading out is usually southwest along Route 66. Heading back is up the California coast to Yosemite, then an every-which-way wander, northeast, southeast, through the Rockies, Yellowstone, the Badlands, the Tetons, Mesa Verde.

We'll start off Day One singing "California here we come" and "Sweet Betsy from Pike." We know all the words, all the verses. The goal of Day One is to get beyond what we consider the boredom of Missouri and Kansas which are too much like Illinois. In other words, a two-lane ride through corn fields along a road that never curves, never mounts a hill, and never dips into a valley.

But after purgatory comes heaven, also known as Oklahoma. When you're in Oklahoma, you know you're somewhere else. You've left your elm-tree-lined, suburban Illinois street behind and entered a postcard panorama. After Oklahoma you cut through a corner of Texas, and later you can brag and say you've been to Texas, then New Mexico and Arizona. Mountains and deserts. Roadside attractions. Indian trading posts and places to stop and see rattlesnakes, petrified wood, cowboy ghost towns, woven Navajo blankets, buffalo, bears.

Dad does most of the driving, with Mom pitching in for an hour or two every day. Mom's main job is navigation, keeping the paper map within reach, unfolding and refolding it as needed, and calculating how far we'll go each day.

Sometimes in the afternoon when we still have several more hours, five or ten or a dozen more towns to travel through, Mom and Dad calculate how many more miles we might wish to go: Seligman to Peach Springs. Peach Springs to Kingman. We listen from the back seat, but don't interrupt the back-and-forth from the front. Mom and Dad's voices, adding the miles in a call and response, is like a secret recitation of a secret code:

Dad: "We just got to Seligman. Let's calculate to Kingman."

Mom: "Okay. Next is Peach Springs. Fifteen miles then twelve."

Dad: "Twenty-seven."

Mom: "Eight more."

Dad: "Thirty-five."

Mom: "Nine."

Dad: "Forty-four."

Mom: "Sixteen."

Dad: "Sixty."

Mom: "That's it."

Dad would announce: "Only a few more miles, kids. Then we stop. How about we play a game."

Here are some of the games we play in the car. There's *Guess how long it takes to go a mile.* Rules: Dad is driving and says, "Ready, set, go." Whenever each of us kids thinks we've gone a mile, we say, "Now!" The winner gets a piece of bubble gum or a Lifesaver.

We also play car bingo with heavy cardboard game cards that have little red plastic windows to slide across each sight you find: a cow, a barn, a truck, a church with a steeple.

We look at license plates and see how many of the forty-eight states we can find. Meg has a notebook and keeps track whenever we see a new one.

Maybe we'll have a limerick challenge.

Maybe we'll play Yatz, throwing the dice in an empty shoebox. Dad plays, too, even though he's driving, usually designating Meg to roll for him because she has the best data reporting skills.

"Dad," she tells him, "you got a six, a five, two twos, and a one."

Dad will answer: "Keep the biggies and roll the rest."

* * *

On the trip where it happened, we had detoured off Route 66 for a night in Las Vegas. We went to a casino and watched Mom and Dad feed coins into slot machines and pull down the handle. They set the betting rule as, *We stop playing when we've lost five dollars.* Our motel was on the edge of the city, away from the bright lights. It was a long single-story structure of connected rooms with metal chairs outside painted pink, yellow, and turquoise blue. The swimming pool was shaped like an arrowhead.

In the swimming pool, Mom was the star. She had gone to a big high school that had a pool paid for with New Deal money, and she knew how to do fancy dives. She'd get a good bounce off the board and do a somersault into the water or a swan dive.

"Watch your Mom," Dad would say. "Isn't she something?"

Dad could swim, but not well. He'd learned with the other company town kids, miners' kids, splashing in the shallows of the Monongahela River while the giant coal barges floated by in the channel, stately, like a row of elephants.

Come late afternoon, a big truck pulled into the motel lot loaded with watermelons, and we got one and ate the whole thing, sitting outside in the afternoon sun. We went to bed early that night. My parents had one double bed, three of us kids shared a second, and one lucky child—usually Meg because she was the oldest—got a rollaway cot. In the bed, my brothers and I slept head-feet-head because otherwise we'd talk and giggle and keep each other awake, and we needed to sleep. We'd leave to cross the desert at 3 a.m.

When the alarm from Mom's wind-up alarm clock rousted us, we pulled on clothes already laid out, while Dad piled the suitcases in the back of the car. Only about ten minutes of consciousness was required for the move from motel bed to car. Dad and Mom were in the front. My sister, brothers, and I sprawled in the second and third seats. Usually, all the passengers succumbed within minutes to the blackness and the sound of the wheels on pavement. Dad kept his eyes on the road and drove fast, out into the desert. The race was on.

I don't know why, on that one trip, I didn't fall asleep. Maybe it was the appeal of one-on-one time with Dad, something precious in a family of six. I was in the second seat, directly behind Mom who was dozing, curled up in a ball, with her sweater over her like a blanket. I scooted forward, leaning my arms on the back of the bench seat in front of me to see out the front windshield. There were no other cars, the night was complete, our headlights the only illumination, outlining for brief instants the cactus and sand and scrub at the shoulder of the road.

"How far will we go today?" I whispered.

"Less than three hundred," Dad answered. "We'll get to Los Angeles nice and early." He kept his voice low, too, so as not to wake the others.

Three hundred was nothing. Usually we'd do five hundred miles in a day. Once we did over seven hundred. It all depended on the stops. There were short stops for gas when Mom gave us nickels and we could pull ice-cold pop in glass bottles from the vending machine. My favorite was Dr. Pepper. At that time it was made with real cane sugar and was only available west of the Mississippi. There were longer stops to explore parks and nature preserves, places to feed donkeys or ride horses.

"When will the sun come up?" I asked.

"Not for a while yet. Can you see the outline of the mountains?"

I looked but couldn't. Only stars above. Only the headlight beams.

It was silent again.

And then it happened.

*Light.*

Light as bright as day, as bright as noon. Light as immediate as switching on a lamp. Light that revealed the desert around us: sand, shrubs, cactus, mountains. All clear, distinct, full of brightness. Color and light.

My father, shocked, turned the wheel as if to avoid something in the road. The car swerved, and we bumped along the shoulder till he regained control and pulled us back onto the pavement.

The others still slept. *Slept!* while Dad and I gazed stunned and in wonder as we sped through that bright-as-noon landscape.

But the light was fading now, slowly, slowly seeping away like the exhalation of a long breath. It was dimmer, shaded, shadowy—as if time had speeded up and was racing through the day, the afternoon, the evening. And then it was gone. The night was upon us again. The sound of the wheels on the pavement was humming again.

"Dad …," I almost couldn't speak, "what was that?"

"The bomb. I forgot it was happening today. The man at the motel desk had a newspaper. He showed me the article. The army is testing an atomic bomb. That was the light."

"But we didn't see a cloud. There wasn't any noise."

"The test site is miles away, sixty-five or seventy miles. It's too far to see anything or hear anything. It's only light that travels so far."

* * *

In the late 1950s, the Nevada Test Site was used to conduct above-ground nuclear weapons tests. For a time, Las Vegas hosted "bomb tourists" who would gather atop the tall hotels to marvel at the light, seemingly safe behind a barrier of desert, miles of desert. They gathered to marvel at the transformation of matter to energy. In the years that followed, it became clear no barrier was adequate, and the tests ended.

The light my father and I saw in the desert—the total erasure of the night—still stays with me more than half a century later. For a time, we could share this memory. Months would pass, or years, but then we'd talk about summer vacations and those road trips and one of us would say, "Do you remember that night in the desert outside Las Vegas? Do you remember the light?" And we'd launch into the tale, trading details, marveling still.

Now my parents are gone. Mom first, then Dad. I'm the sole eyewitness. Because of that, I'm putting this memory down on paper to save it as something authentic. Something marvelous but not fantasy. Amazing but not fanciful.

I crossed the desert in 1958, and a silent bomb stole the night and the pinpoint sparkle of stars, sped up time, illuminated sand and mountains, then receded like a wave, leaving us again in the comfort of darkness.

I can tell you this from experience. I can tell you this as a witness. I can tell you this in wonder and yet with the hope, the hope against hope, that never again will there be witnesses to such a creation, a creation meant to destroy.

# Field Trip

"It's a little hard to explain," Kyle said. He fidgeted in his seat.

"Try."

"It might take a while. It's complicated."

Mr. Evans pressed his lips together in disapproval. "*It's complicated?* We're not talking about a Gen Z relationship here. We're talking about how a day trip, which was supposed to involve a morning at the mall and a lunch at Italian Garden, turned into an expedition to God knows where and the return of a half-dozen giggling, intoxicated, AWOL senior citizens to the Maple Grove Residences at two in the morning."

"Actually, it was a little closer to two-thirty," Kyle said. He knew he'd have to face the music with regard to yesterday's Maple Grove field trip, and since he had to spill the beans on the whole thing, he felt he might as well be honest.

"And not everyone was drinking," Kyle added. "I didn't touch a drop myself. I wouldn't, you know. When I drive the van I stick to the rules, hundred percent. My boss, Ms. Kitty—I mean, you know, Mrs. Kittridge—is super strict on that, and I gotta agree. When people rent a van or bus from Magic Carpet Conveyances, they're entitled to a *Safe and Sensational* trip. That's the company motto: *Safe and Sensational.*"

Mr. Evans scowled. Leaning back in his leather office chair, he crossed his arms. "Then perhaps you should enlighten me about what happened, where you were, and why I received a phone call in the middle of the night complaining about a group of rowdies waking up our residents on Sunshine Lane."

"Those weren't rowdies, sir. I mean the folks I dropped off *are* residents. It's just that the main gate was closed, so I couldn't do the drop offs right at the bungalows like I usually do. So Theo said, 'Let's just get out and walk,' and the other folks agreed, and we all got out of the van. Me too because I wanted to make sure they got home safe. Our motto, you know, is—"

"Safe and Sensational, yes, you told me."

"Well, as we were heading down the street, Theo and Nick put their arms around each other and started singing 'Little Brown Jug,' and before I knew it the whole group was singing along with them."

Kyle could tell Mr. Evans was losing patience. Not that he had much of that admirable quality. Mr. Evans wasn't his favorite client, even if he was the head of the outfit that managed the whole Maple Grove community, and even though Maple Grove booked tons of vans and buses from Magic Carpet. Kyle thought Mr. Evans spent way too much time in his wood-paneled office, and not nearly enough with the people that actually lived in the retirement community. Still, he knew Magic Carpet didn't want to lose this important client, so he had agreed to this conversation after Ms. Kitty had received the complaint.

"Try to smooth things over," she had told him. "Evans gets his feathers ruffled way too easy, but it takes all kinds, I guess. He's really got no reason to complain. It's not like we charge him overtime for the extra hours. Our deal is flat rate per trip. And ...," she had given Kyle a grin, "I have to say, from what you told me, it sounds like everyone had a grand time."

Mr. Evans' voice brought Kyle back to the present. *"Why don't you start at the beginning. Tell me exactly what happened."*

It didn't escape Kyle's notice that the older man was speaking slowly, in a loud voice, like he was speaking to a child.

"Okay," Kyle said. *"Here's what we did after I picked up Theo, Nick, Howie, and the three ladies. Nancy, Tillie, and Mary Jo."* He had matched Mr. Evans' slow, deliberate cadence.

"The whole party got on board promptly at ten, just like I was expecting. Ms. Kitty told me there would only be six because some of the regular ladies that go to the mall were headed to the flower show, so it would be a smaller group than normal.

"As per usual, we pull outside the gate, and I'm heading for the highway, when Theo asks can I maybe pull over into the gas station. I figure somebody forgot to hit the bathroom before taking off, and I pull into the Texaco station, and turn off the engine.

"Then Theo says, 'Kyle, my boy'—he talks like that, you know— 'Kyle, my boy, we want to suggest a little change of plans. It just so happens that today's the day that Nick's grandson is playing ball at the state regional semifinal game over at the college. And he would love to see the game. In fact all of us would love to see the game. And none of us would love to see the mall.' Then Tillie pipes in and says that her cousin owns this really great barbecue stand that does baskets for tailgating parties, and they'd ordered one of the deluxe carry-outs already, and she hopes I like ribs with coleslaw on the side because that's what they'd ordered for me."

Kyle could tell that Mr. Evans wasn't too happy to hear this. Ms. Kitty had told him she suspected he was getting a kickback from the Italian Garden manager for steering all the day trips to his particular site. Kyle suspected that it was just a matter of Mr. Evans not having much of an imagination. Kyle liked Italian Garden just fine, but who wants to eat at the same place every time you're out on the town? If you could even call a field trip to the mall being "out on the town." Kyle sensed that maybe he should hurry through his explanation of what happened the next couple hours.

He took a deep breath and started in, explaining that they had picked up the basket from Tillie's cousin who told them he'd tucked in some potato salad along with the coleslaw and put in a big batch of chocolate chip cookies to boot. Then they'd headed off to the game which had gone into extra innings but ended up in a win for Nick's grandson's team which meant there'd be a trip upstate for the regional collegiate final. And everyone was in such a celebratory mood that it seemed a shame to head back to Maple Grove because, as Theo said, the night was young, there was champagne to order, and dancing to be done.

"I checked in with Ms. Kitty, of course," Kyle assured Mr. Evans. "When she found out that Theo made the suggestion, she said I should just, you know, go with the flow. That Theo knew what he was doing, and a good time would be had by all."

Kyle thought maybe he shouldn't tell Mr. Evans that Ms. Kitty had laughed when she gave the go-ahead on Theo's change of plans and remarked, almost to herself, "I love that man."

"We ended up at this cool place at the edge of town," Kyle said. "There were some of the baseball players celebrating with hamburgers and French fries, and a band was playing, and pretty soon everyone was out on the dance floor." He smiled to himself thinking about Theo and Tillie cutting a rug. When a slow dance came on, Theo had pulled her close, Tillie had wrapped her arms around his neck, and the two of them had swayed together in time to the music.

"I think everyone had a really, really nice time," Kyle concluded. "And got home safe and sound." Kyle had indeed made sure his passengers made it home, walking each of them to their door. Well, Theo didn't get back to his place because Tillie had invited him in for a nightcap, but Kyle thought that piece of news wasn't any of Mr. Evans' business.

"Is there anything else you need to know?" Kyle asked. "'Cause Ms. Kitty needs me to help her with the schedule for next month."

Mr. Evans didn't look happy. He had a kind of half-frown, half-scowl, disapproving expression on his face. But after a pause, he waved his hand in dismissal.

Kyle grinned, got to his feet, and put his new baseball cap back on his head. Theo had bought souvenir caps for the whole group. He was looking forward to getting back to the office. Ms. Kitty said Theo wanted to do a party bus rental for the regional final game coming up just two weeks from now. It was going to be safe. And sensational.

# Gathering Hay

Katie studied the painting. "Grandmother, look at this one. I might pick this one for my homework." She pointed to the glossy image on the page of the large book in front of her.

"What's the assignment?" Ella asked.

"The art teacher said to find a picture where there were people doing something outside. Then we're supposed to write our *opinion*. You know, what we like and what we don't like and what we *think* about it. She said now that we're in fifth grade, we could start to *critique* art, and she explained that doing a critique isn't the same thing as being *critical*. It's kinda like analyzing it."

Ella poured boiling water from the kettle into her cup, dunked the tea bag up and down for a minute, then brought the cup to the kitchen table. She pulled out a chair and sat down next to the child. Katie pushed the open book over to Ella and pointed at the painting depicting three peasants seated by a loosely gathered pile of hay. Two of the figures were female. One reclined against the hay as if ready to enjoy a nap, the other had her hands drawn together in her lap. A young man sat with them, a plain brown hat upon his head, one hand resting on a drawn-up knee. Near the group was a basket with a cloth folded neatly over its top.

"What do you like about this?" Ella asked.

"I like that they have a big basket. It looks like a picnic basket, and maybe they're going to have a picnic. I like that. And the lady lying down looks like she's kind of happy to relax. I feel like that when I'm lying in the hammock outside. All sort of dreamy."

"What's the painting called?" Ella asked.

Katie squinted down at the fine print. "This says *Gathering Hay*, and it says it was painted in 1890 by … Ist-van C-sok. I don't know if that's how you say it. He was from a country called *Hungry*."

"Hun*gary*," Ella said. "It's in Europe."

"Is it near where your grandmother came from?" Katie knew her grandmother's family had arrived on a ship a long, *long* time ago from Europe.

"My family came from a place called Prussia," Ella explained. It's part of Germany. And when this painting was done, Hungary was part of Austria. And Austro-Hungary shared a border with Germany. They were close, but not that close." She laughed and took a sip of tea. "I'm not explaining this very well."

Katie nodded wisely. "I know it's sorta complicated. In the library at school there are all these maps, and they have dates on them because the librarian said that the countries were different at different times."

"Is there anything you don't like in the painting?" Ella asked.

Katie studied the picture again, then looked up. "It's not like I think anything's ugly or bad. It's just …."

"What?"

"Well, the title of the picture says they're gathering hay. So that's like their job. And maybe they're on their lunch break or something, and that's why they have a picnic basket. But if I was working outside, I wouldn't wear a pretty dress, like my yellow dress with the hearts on it, but both of the ladies in the picture have pretty clothes on. Like the one lying down has a flowered skirt and the other lady has an even fancier skirt that's kind of lacy, and a blouse with ruffles around her face. I wouldn't wear pretty clothes like that if I had to do work outside. I mean they have aprons on, but that won't really keep their clothes all the way clean."

"Back then, people didn't have lots of clothes," Ella pointed out. "Not if they lived on a farm. They wouldn't have a closet full of outfits — so many outfits to choose from that it sometimes takes a little too long to get ready for school in the morning, and a girl might almost miss the bus while she's deciding whether to wear her pink sweater or her blue one or the one with the kittens on the pockets."

Katie giggled then turned from the book to look at her grandmother. Ella's gray hair was pulled up into a bun. Her eyes seemed slightly enlarged behind her thick spectacles.

"Grandmother, was it that way when you were young? Like it shows in this picture? On the farm in Indiana?"

Ella didn't want to think about the farm in Indiana, but the child's question sent her back. Back to when she was wearing an old pair of trousers handed down from one of her brothers. Her plain skirt and single dress were reserved for school and church. Then just for church because when she completed primary school her father had deemed her education finished.

"Primary school is enough," he had told her. "High school you don't need." He had said it in that way that told her he wouldn't change his mind. He had said the same to the teacher who'd ridden out to the farm in a failed effort to get Ella's parents to reconsider and allow Ella to continue her education.

"Primary school is enough." She could hear those words like it was yesterday. They still, for a moment, had the power to stop her heart, to make a wail of despair echo in her brain.

"She is needed here," her father had said to the teacher. And that was that. The farm was poor, there were too many children, so the children's hands were needed—to work in the fields, feed the animals, prepare food at the wood-burning stove, haul water in buckets from the well, scrub in an always failing effort to stay clean.

"Grandmother?"

Katie's voice brought her back. The smoke-blackened walls of the farmhouse were replaced. She was once more in the cheerful kitchen, with its blue Formica counters and lacy white curtains. The sink and stove were spotless. Last year, she purchased a dishwasher. A small shelf in the corner held Katie's schoolbooks.

"Do you know what the word 'idealized' means?" she asked the girl.

Katie shook her head.

"It means that something—like this picture of working on a farm— is made to seem better than it really is. It's made to seem happier and easier."

"So, if it's *idealized* it's kind of like a lie?"

"Well, maybe it's what the painter wished it was like—working on a farm. Or hoped it could be like. And there might be some truth mixed in and some part that's just his imagination."

"There can be good lies, Grandmother. Like when I told Nate I thought he was getting much better at baseball even though I didn't really think he was. But I wanted to encourage him instead of make him feel bad. But lots of lies are bad."

Ella nodded. "Yes, lots of lies are bad."

"How do you spell *idealized*?" Katie picked up her pencil.

Ella repeated the letters, and Katie copied them carefully onto the paper.

"Are you ready to start your homework now?"

"Yes, I think I am."

"If you finish before your mom and dad get home, you can read it out to me. I'd like to hear what you have to say. I'm interested in your *critique*."

Katie smiled and began to write.

# Vamp

He'd never know how close he came to immortality last week in that walk-in freezer. Vampires prefer the cold, after all, and I was damn hungry, having made do with a few bites of raw hamburger meat and a couple pieces of uncooked pork I'd filched early that morning before the rest of the crew came in to start up the smoker and heat up the grill. Oh Lordy, I was tempted all right, but—contrary to what you read in pulp fiction and all that old-timey horror stuff—vamps aren't heartless.

And we don't skulk around sinking our teeth into the necks of every poor soul that crosses our path. Putting morality aside—and I never, in real life, put morality aside except for the sake of an argument, like I'm laying out for you here—murder just doesn't cut it as a way to meet our dietary preferences. That decision was made in our community ages and ages ago. Murder's way too messy and attracts the cops. It attracts the media, too, which is worse. And face it, it's not really necessary given that the urge to go vegan has only enthralled about five percent of the population. Contrast that with the half million people that have jobs in production, packing, importing, sales, and direct distribution of meat and poultry products. And if you get to the meat before it gets to the heat, you've got all the liquid red you'll need.

Think about it. Meat is everywhere. If you get the urge, even if you're in the middle of Kansas or hiking through the Adirondacks or soaking up the rays along the California coast, you're never going to be all that far from a diner or fast-food joint that'll have burgers on the menu. Yeah, you usually have to come up with a story about why you want the patty outa the fridge not offa the grill, but that's why vamps developed good storytelling skills. And like I said, we've got scruples, as good as those of the average man on the street—maybe a little better when you consider scruples are at issue every time you take a bite.

I mean, we're not like those elegant, high-brow characters in *Twilight*, for god's sake. Yeah, those books and movies corrected the record on a coupla things, but everyone already knew vamps don't spontaneously combust in the sunlight. We don't *like* it, but I know a boatload of humans that don't like it either. And let's get real. Tanning is bad for your skin. And while the *Twilight* vamps didn't set off fire alarms in the dawn's early light, they got all glittery-glow when the sun came up. It's all of a piece with how a lot of modern writers portray vamps as pretty damn *refined*, living in big fancy houses, and playing the piano.

I remember sitting around with a couple old Bela Lugosi guys smoking cigarettes, reading some of the juicier passages out loud and hooting at how goddam pretty and romantic it all was supposed to be. Most of us actually have to make a living, you know, work the 9-to-5 or the late shift at the factory or check folks out at Walmart to pay the bills. Or do like I did and take a job waitressing at a barbecue joint.

Still, like I said, vamps, even blue-collar vamps, aren't without feelings. And that boy sure can kiss. And make me laugh, even, right in the middle of it all. He thinks I'm funny, and he grins at what he thinks is my kinky side—my natural preference for lovemaking in the cold. When I first signed onto this waitress gig it was December, and our first night together it was January. I opened the window wide to see the moonlight sparkle on the icicles hanging along the eaves and at the edge of the fire escape. He asked why I didn't have a single warm blanket, and I said, "Who the hell needs one?" and we laughed and had a grand old time.

But now it's August, and everyone wants barbecue in August. Don't ask me why. I totally get the crowd at Dairy Queen and Frosty's, the intoxication that comes from shaved ice and frozen treats in every color of the rainbow. But the smoke and fire of a barbecue joint just isn't my idea of where you head on a blistering day in the summer.

So why do I stay? Well, summer won't last forever. And all that red meat arrives right on schedule in refrigerated trucks. And I can make a dozen trips a day into the walk-in freezer to refresh my spirit while I haul out fries and pie and steak and ribs. And, yeah, I'll admit it, that boy sure can kiss.

# Sidewalk Sale

"Okay, Mr. Bello, I checked the weather report, and it's going to be really nice all weekend long, so I think we can put a lot of stuff outside for the sidewalk sale. and we won't have to worry about rain."

"I told you, kid, just call me Joe. Everyone calls me Joe."

The kid got a stubborn look on his face. Joe recognized it from a few previous exchanges they'd had and wondered, first, how a scrawny teenaged boy with a long nose and a shock of black hair could express so many complicated emotions just by twisting his face around. Second, he wondered why he had agreed to take him on in the first place.

He actually had an answer to that second point. Everyone knew that, come June, the high school guidance counselor morphed into an absolute tiger when it came to finding full-time employment or part-time jobs or paid internships or whatever for all the kids that weren't sailing on to college. He'd known the guidance counselor forever. They'd actually been high school classmates way back when. She'd been a popular girl, smart, gone on to teachers college, married the boy she'd gone steady with in high school, then went into guidance when her own kids were born.

He'd known, even back then, that she was a tiger when it came to taking up a cause or fighting for what she thought was right. He'd been expecting a call from her as the summer began, so hadn't been surprised to hear her voice.

"Joe, hi, it's Melanie."

"Hiya, Melanie, what's doing?"

"Congratulations on opening up at your new location. I heard all about you taking over Flanagan's Furnishings and combining it with your repair business. I saw the article the Chamber did on you in its newsletter."

"Thank you, Mel. And now that the pleasantries are over, who do you want me to hire?"

She laughed. She had an infectious laugh, which he thought must have helped her in all the years she'd worked, with all the teens she'd worked with, and all the administrators she'd worked for and worked around.

After the conversation, he'd agreed to hire the kid. Michael Maggio. "Yes," Melanie had said, "he's one of *those* Maggios, but this kid is different. He's nothing like his older brothers. You'll like him. He's full of energy, full of ideas, talks a mile a minute, and doesn't have a mean bone in his body. And Sarah Abrams said to tell you he's a gem."

"Sarah says all the kids are gems," he'd replied.

But the mention of Sarah's name had sealed the deal. He liked Sarah. She hadn't grown up in town, only arrived about a year ago. She taught English at the high school, and he'd seen her at the farmer's market, and she'd volunteered at the Community Clean-Up Day. She'd even come by his shop a time or two. She'd bought a desk from him and a bookshelf. He'd delivered them to the bungalow she'd purchased on Porter Street. They'd chatted and laughed. He'd admired the new garden she'd started out back.

Now, when they saw each other around town, they stopped and smiled and there was more talk. One early Saturday morning, they had, by chance, both turned up at the diner at the same time, so they shared a booth and chatted over coffee and orange juice and scrambled eggs.

The kid's voice brought him back to business.

"Calling you 'Joe' is fine for your regular customers, Mr. Bello. But I'm your employee. And I think calling you 'Mr. Bello' sets a real nice professional tone especially when people come into the shop who are, like, out-of-town people that drive up here for a weekend in the country. And we're going to get a whole lot of people like that this weekend because it's Saturday-Sunday Sidewalk Sale. And we want to attract people who are, you know, shopping for antiques and are interested in wandering around this nice, big, old-fashioned building looking for something special. Like they're on a treasure hunt."

"That's why you had me put up the big sign outside the shop advertising 'Antiques'? You don't think people would stop in with just the regular sign over the door?"

"Well … Joe's Junk Shop doesn't have quite the same appeal. You know, broad appeal. You know, like for marketing and branding."

"It's Joe's Joyful Junk Shop. I always thought the word 'Joyful' added that little bit of whimsy that was needed to pull in the customers."

The kid saw he was kidding and saw he had won the argument, and his face untwisted itself, and a grin appeared. "Should we go over everything then?"

"You're the boss."

"Um, actually, you're the boss. When I told Ms. Abrams that I got the job here she said to me that sometimes smart people can get a little bossy, and it's important to keep people with you instead of putting them off, and if you listen to other people you'll often see that they're smart, too, and you can, like, learn things and mutually appreciate each other."

The kid's face was twisted into another one of those interesting expressions. "Ms. Abrams does that, you know. She gives you a compliment about something while telling you at the same time how you can improve yourself."

"Sarah … um … Ms. Abrams is a pretty smart lady herself."

"She is," the kid agreed. "So here's what I think we should do today to get ready for the sale …."

What followed was a rather detailed discussion of how best to display the shop's wares. Only furniture would go outside because that was most likely to attract the city-folk antique buyers. Glassware and pottery would stay inside where they were less likely to be broken, although especially nice pieces would be arranged in one of the windows.

"We've got some really good vases, Rosevilles and McCoys," the kid said. "I looked all the patterns up online and made little information cards about them that we can put in the display. And we've got Fiestaware, too, which is still really popular. And we can put the pottery with some of the older quilts and needlework pieces that are from the same era. We've also got that really old, but really nice teddy bear, that we can put on one of the quilts. And maybe the little lamp with the stained-glass shade and that stereoscope we got in last month with the collection of viewer cards in the wooden box. All those things will get people interested.

"What about the other window?" Joe asked. "Right now we've got hand tools and kitchenware."

"I think we should change it up," the kid said decisively. "This weekend it's all about what will bring in the out-of-town big spenders looking for a bargain. But not like an eggbeater bargain."

"That pipe wrench probably won't spark much interest either."

The kid grinned.

"Folks will be looking for *treasure*," Joe said. "It's your word, and I think it's the right one."

"Yep, so we should go with jewelry."

Joe nodded. "Exactly what I was going to say, though most of what we have isn't super high-end stuff."

"Yeah, but city people go to Tiffany's or something for that. We've got really nice costume jewelry from the 1930s and 40s. And some vintage pieces that are just pretty and unusual, even if the diamonds are small or a little bit imperfect. There's that gold locket in the shape of a heart like women used to wear. It's got a rose engraved on it instead of initials so anyone can wear it. We've got some charm bracelets, too. Lots of sterling silver pins. People will like that stuff because it's old."

Joe nodded his head. He had seen that happen with customers, many older, but some younger, too. "Do you know why I think that happens? I think they know an older piece of jewelry comes with a story. Even if you don't know the story, you know it's been worn by someone, maybe given as a gift to a sweetheart, so it's like it carries good luck or something."

Joe stopped, a little embarrassed, but the kid was nodding his head sagely. He eyed the older man. "You know …,"

"What?"

"When Ms. Abrams came by the shop last week, we, uh, talked a little. I think she wanted to make sure I was doing okay. She listened to all my ideas about the sidewalk sale and said she thought they sounded wonderful. She said … well, she said you were the *perfect person* for me to work with because you were smart and nice and really listened to other people."

"That was real nice of her to say," Joe said, and felt a lightness in his heart that he realized he hadn't felt for quite a few years.

The kid examined his boss. "You know, Ms. Abrams looked at that locket, the heart-shaped one, and said she thought it was real pretty. I think she's planning to come by during the sale because she wants to see how all my plans worked out and how the store looks. And I think she just kinda likes to come by here. Maybe we could put that locket in the window but not sell it. Maybe we could say it's kinda *spoken for*?"

Joe grinned. "Good idea, kid. Now let's start getting some of the furniture out front. I think this treasure hunt's going to work out just fine."

# Dreams

It was Annalee's last night on the chorus line, so Cath and Babs were treating her. The spot they had chosen was across the street, around the corner, and down a couple blocks from the hotel-casino. They'd been there before, and knew it was good. It was a modest place, homey, and open all night. Not open all night in order to pick up business from the high rollers and revelers in evening wear. It was open to cater to those that worked the long hours, waited on the tables, made up the rooms, served the drinks, prepared the food that went into the chafing dishes on the buffet tables, sold cigarettes, or sold themselves.

They chose it because there they could find a good sandwich or a hot meal. Homemade soup. Homemade pie. Excellent coffee in a heavy mug. Soda pop with red-and-white striped straws. A smile from Tommaso who owned the joint and knew everyone's name.

"You're going to miss us, aren't you?" Cath said as they settled into a booth.

"I'll miss you like the dickens, but we'll still see each other. I'm just going to finish up my high school. I'm not going to the moon."

"Maybe she will go to the moon," Babs said. "President Kennedy said, 'We choose to go to the moon and do other things, not because they are easy, but because they are hard.' He said choosing hard things is the best way to challenge ourselves and measure our energies and skills."

Annalee laughed. "Just finishing up my high school is going to be hard enough. The math part won't be too bad because that was always something I could do. But I have to do English, too. I remember when we were given sentences to diagram, and I would just stare at the paper and not be able to make heads or tails of it. And writing essays, I'm just not good at that. I can never think of anything to write about."

Cath pursed her lips. "After the last couple years working at The Silver Horseshoe, I'd think you'd have plenty to write about. Maybe those essays were hard before because you hadn't seen enough of the world, so you didn't have enough to say."

"Working as a dancer in one sorta medium-sized, Las Vegas hotel and casino is not seeing the world. Seeing the world is New York City. Seeing the world is Paris."

Babs laughed. "Yes, those would be wonderful. And I'll bet you'll get to those places one day. But I think Cath is right, too. Think of what we've been through together. Remember when that soldier boy who'd been stationed in Germany won the Jackpot and gave every girl a hundred dollars because he said we were all his lucky charms?"

"Remember when that guy from California said he was scouting around for the next big Hollywood star?" Cath said.

"He was scouting all right," Annalee said, "but more likely for the bedroom, not the movie set."

"I remember when we all hid Marcie's marriage for a whole two years because Asshole Albert said any girl that got married would get fired. Then when he finally found out, we said we'd quit—all of us—if he fired her, and he had to back down. That was *sweet*. I remember him getting all red in the face, and huffing and puffing, and then just walking out because he knew he was beat." Babs sighed. "You know, Marcie's baby's due next summer. Gosh, I miss her. Hey, you should talk to her. I bet she'd help you with your G.E.D. She didn't start dancing until after high school, and I heard she was a pretty good student."

Tommaso appeared at their booth and began placing items from his tray onto the table. "I've got everything set for your celebration, ladies," he announced. "Hamburger sandwiches, French fries, Coca-Cola, and cake for dessert. My boy did the baking this morning. Chocolate cake with chocolate frosting, right?"

"Tommaso, is Marcello here tonight?"

"He's here tonight and here for good! He's going to help me run this place now that I'm getting to be an old geezer. He said he'd spent enough years in an army uniform, and it was time to put on an apron."

"Oh, how nice for you," Babs said. "And for him. What a dream come true."

"I think it's a night to celebrate dreams," Cath said, raising her glass. "Here's to all our dreams."

They clinked their glasses, and drank the bubbly soda, and laughed.

"Dreams can come true, can't they?" Annalee said.

"You bet they can," Tommaso said. "Take it from me. We geezers know a thing or two about hamburgers, chocolate cake, and dreams."

# Bus Ride

Nellie checked her watch then stuck her hands back in the pockets of her coat and turned her back to the cold wind coming off the lake. Only eight more minutes to stand in the early morning chill. She knew the bus would be on time because the bus was a "green limousine," a giant Chicago Transit Authority bus, and her stop, right near Lake Michigan, was a regular stop, and—most importantly—her driver was Benny, and Benny was never late. She didn't know how he did it. Rush-hour, weekday traffic might get snarled, there might be a fender bender on Lake Shore Drive, a water main might break and flood all lanes, but somehow Benny was never late. Even on St. Patrick's Day when Mayor Daley had the Chicago River dyed green and thousands of tourists arrived to raise a glass in celebration and kiss each other because everyone was Irish.

Bennie would pull up, open the doors with a swish, grin, and say what he always said: "Welcome aboard ladies and gents."

Benny had a good grin. A good look altogether, she thought. He was as old as she was, she figured, past fifty, but he looked like his half-century-and-more had been pretty well filled with a hell of a lot more than just driving a bus. Things like wrestling maybe, or prize fighting. His nose was crooked enough to give evidence of at least one break. His eyes were blue, his hair black with some gray coming in, and, when he grinned, a gold tooth could be seen.

If Benny wasn't driving, who knew when the bus would arrive. But she'd been riding this route long enough to know that Benny was rarely sick and usually took his two weeks off in the summer. Last summer she had marked her calendar on the first day when a substitute driver was on duty, so she knew when Benny would be back on the job. He'd grinned when he'd seen her, and, after his welcome to all the "ladies and gents," he'd directed her to a space on the front seat right behind him.

"Sit near me, Nellie-dear," he'd said.

"Do you have tales for me?" she'd asked.

"Ah, so many tales, but I'm not sure they're fit for a fine lady's ears."

"Then you can definitely tell me, and I definitely want to hear them," she'd said, and they'd laughed.

The stories that followed were always grand. Like how he'd gone west on his vacation, first stop Mount Rushmore. "Always wanted to see it for myself," he'd said, "ever since I saw that Hitchcock picture—"

"*North by Northwest,*" she finished for him. "Always one of my favorites. Better than *Psycho.*"

"I had to hide my face in my hands for that one," he said with a shudder, "scared the living daylights outa me."

She snorted at that. "Hah. You probably just took another handful of popcorn and waited for Anthony Perkins to get his comeuppance. But tell me about Mount Rushmore."

"It was splendid," he'd said and went on to describe the famous monument. He'd reflected on whether Teddy Roosevelt's accomplishments had been in the same league as Washington's and Jefferson's and Lincoln's, and they'd had a debate about who they'd include if another such monument were being planned now. He favored Kennedy. They went back and forth on Ike. They both agreed on FDR.

Her bus ride was thirty-five minutes long, so they always had time for a nice chat, although it was punctuated at every stop as Benny opened the doors and welcomed each new group of riders. He knew all the regulars and would often greet them by name or exchange a word or two.

"Can you believe the Cubbies gave away the game last weekend? You could hear the wails from Wrigley Field all over the city."

Or, "You seen the Apollo 8 capsule yet? They've brought it to the Museum of Science and Industry."

Or, "That new city council guy better be careful, or come winter, Mayor Daley won't send the snowplows into his district."

Sometimes there were new riders who would ask directions or riders who'd ask for a paper transfer because they needed to take two different buses to get to work.

Nellie felt lucky that Benny's bus stopped right in front of her place of employment, the Queen of Clean Laundromat. Not many people would consider her job that important or a good *career choice.* Is that what they called it these days? But Nellie thought it suited her just fine.

The owners, Mr. and Mrs. Farley, were decent and fair and—once they realized how reliable she was, paid her well. There was a chair she could sit on in between helping customers operate the machines. And the customers liked her, and she passed on helpful hints, telling the college kids not to wash red items with white and teaching countless others—young and old—how to fold a fitted sheet.

A cold breeze blew off the lake. Winter would be here soon. Chicago basically had only two real seasons, summer and winter, with an odd week or so in between. They were in the summer to winter transition now.

The breeze moved the clouds and the sun appeared. And like magic, right on time, the bus pulled up. With a whoosh, the doors opened and there was Benny. "Welcome aboard, ladies and gents."

As she climbed the steps, he gave her a grin. "Sit near me, Nellie-dear."

There was a pause as she settled into the seat. The door whooshed closed. He glanced over his shoulder, and, for just a moment, their eyes met.

She felt a little shot of happiness, right in her heart. "Do you have tales for me today, Benny?"

He pulled the bus into traffic. "Always, Nellie-dear, always. So many tales, so many tales …."

# Moving Forward

Dear Celestine,

I am moving forward well in my training here at the Providence School for Secretaries. I have already developed some aptitude with the typewriter, and, after initial struggles, am beginning to acquire skill at stenography. Writing in shorthand is somewhat challenging, but I am determined to succeed. Ah, Cissy, wouldn't we have had such fun as children if we had known shorthand? We could have composed secret messages to each other with no fear of one of our teachers or siblings or parents intercepting our notes and translating our words.

While these skills are not as interesting to me as the readings in history and literature that I enjoyed in high school, I recognize that I am fortunate as I need not seek employment in a factory or in some domestic capacity. And acquiring secretarial skills will not require an extended and expensive period of training as would be necessary if I wished to become a nurse or teacher.

As you have inquired about the matter, I must tell you that living with Aunt Florence has required some period of adjustment. I am sure Mama relayed an imperfect description of my character when she wrote our aunt asking if I might reside with her here in Providence. I know I am something of a disappointment to Mama who had rather hoped Mr. Bartholomew and I might make a match of it, thus settling my future. But after such an arrangement failed to materialize, and, in searching about for some other way to secure my future, she became convinced that work in a secretarial position was the goal I should aspire to since it is a respectable way for an unmarried woman to earn a living. The only obstacle Mama was then required to overcome was the need for a place to reside here in Rhode Island. I am convinced that when importuning Aunt Florence, Mama did not let a truthful but unflattering portrait of my behavior interfere with her plan.

What has been a surprise to me, dearest Cissy, is that I believe there may have been a degree of misapprehension on Mama's part. From the stories she has told of Aunt Florence, I always imagined Papa's older sister to be a rather strict and straitlaced matron, someone who would be rather dour in both manner and appearance.

After being here for only a few weeks, I have become convinced that our understanding of Aunt Florence was not accurate in some interesting particulars. I knew this immediately upon arrival when I first set eyes upon her. It entered my head that there may have been some mistake, and I had been escorted to the wrong address and ushered into a stranger's parlour. My only image of Aunt Florence was from that framed portrait upon the mantel. The woman in that picture was dressed in a fine but rather plain gown and had her hair pinned up in the normal fashion. The woman who greeted me was much older, of course, but looked far different. Cissy, her hair is bobbed. And she was wearing trousers. Not the bloomers or knickerbockers worn by those who wish to exercise or ride a bicycle. *Trousers* such as a man might wear, but not exactly. It is hard to describe. She looked rather pretty, or *dashing*, you might say.

I know that some of those women who are working in factories to aid the war effort have bobbed their hair and donned boilersuits, but it is apparel of a kind I did not expect to see on a wealthy older woman relaxing at her leisure at home.

It is not solely Florence's appearance that is remarkable to me. As I soon came to realize, the view our dear Papa had of his sister was shaped by very early memories that, due to distance and his untimely passing, never had a chance to be revised. One must bear in mind that Papa's experience of the world had not yet seen bobbed hair, bloomers, or boilersuits.

He *had* seen women who had joined the suffragist cause, and although he voiced doubts about such a movement, he was not among those who dismissed such sentiments out of hand. Perhaps my fondness for our father, and enduring grief at his death, have led me to the conviction that he would, in time, have supported votes for women. In any event, I choose to believe that is what would have happened had he not been struck down too early in life.

As you must have surmised by now, Florence is a suffragist. When she entertains those friends who share this commitment, there is more than one woman with bobbed hair and trousers sitting at her ease in the drawing room. The gentlemen who have, at times, attended these gatherings, like Mr. Clayton who is as committed to the cause as is his wife, Doris, do not seem nonplussed by these women's manner of dress.

I want you to know that Aunt Florence and her friends have been very kind to me and have asked so many questions about my secretarial lessons. Then they have the most amusing debates about my "career" as they call it. Some of the ladies are strongly of the opinion that secretarial education will advance women's equality within the business world and open up a pathway to more important duties. Aunt Florence and her special friend Miss Henderson believe the challenge will be whether an employer will reward a talented female secretary or simply regard her as an employee that is less expensive than a man.

In all, I am finding my new circumstances quite interesting. I feel something akin to how Dorothy must have felt after being lifted up into the cyclone and transported to the Land of Oz. There is something unusual and noteworthy to capture my attention at every new turn of the road. Do you remember the fun we used to have reading those books?

Please write me soon, dear Cissy. I am most anxious to hear all the news from home. Your letters are among the brightest spots in my day, and I eagerly look for the arrival of the post, hoping you will have had time to pen me another note.

Your sister,
Adelaide

# Fame and Other Stuff

I don't think it's fair that Martin and I have to write essays as a punishment for handing out flyers and organizing a sit-down strike in front of the school yearbook office. We both felt really, really strongly that part of the yearbook had to be changed, but the editors didn't even want to discuss it or have a vote because we're junior staff and not seniors yet. I think they were just afraid they'd lose the vote. So Martin and I thought we could kind of make things more public and start a bigger conversation in the school community.

Even though things got a little heated when the editors tried to step over us, and we linked arms and started singing "Solidarity Forever," what happened in the hallway was just sort of a "free exchange of ideas" like Dr. Forrest in history class is always saying we should have because that's what the founders were trying to set up. And freedom of speech is in the First Amendment to the Constitution. There's actually five rights in that one single amendment, and I think a lot of them apply to what happened. Like the right to assemble and the right to petition for a redress of grievances. And Martin and I had grievances we wanted to redress, so we assembled and used free speech. And sit-down strikes have been around since 1936, and that's how the United Auto Workers got going. Dr. Forrest talked about that too.

My best friend Lacey is always telling me that I get too upset about stuff, and I should just learn to chill and take a deep breath, but even though I love Lacey, she's gone a little bit too far into that mindfulness stuff and even spent fifty-five dollars of her babysitting money to get acupressure point massage rings that you put on your hands and they're supposed to keep you calm. I think that's what my mother would call *baloney*. Mom says if you want to be calm, do what *her* granny told her to do which is drink some chamomile tea. Mom says there's scientific research and stuff that shows that her granny was right, and chamomile tea doesn't make you spend fifty-five dollars.

She also says that anything that costs a lot of money and is promoted by a famous movie star or a model and isn't based in science isn't a good way to stay calm. Plus, she says sometimes people have to *stop* being calm and get off their butts and do something like her granny used to do when she was walking a picket line for the union.

Excuse my use of the word "butts." I'm only quoting my mom who says things without lots of embellishments. We talked about this in English class, and Ms. Marshall says it's okay to use a swear or an inappropriate word as long as you're quoting or it's really necessary.

So here's what happened. It's kind of related to what my mom said about not buying stuff just because a famous person is selling it. And it's kind of related to the whole idea of being famous. In high school, there's different ways for people to be famous for different stuff. Like the kids who are in the talent show or the spring musical are famous. Or if you're on the football team or the basketball team or you make the cheerleading squad, you're famous. Or you get elected to the student council. Or you're the prom queen which our high school still has even though it's kind of dopey and even though a couple years ago they supposedly changed it, so it wasn't based on looks. Everyone knows it's still a popularity contest, and a pretty girl will get picked and get famous that way.

Well, usually I ignore a lot of that stuff, and it doesn't make me upset. But when Martin and I found out about the yearbook editors using the same categories again for tagging people in the *Superlatives* section of the yearbook—you know, like best dressed and best sense of humor and best smile and most likely to succeed—we decided we had to do something about it.

Especially because that list is the *only* thing in the yearbook that could be more open to more kids and kind of get updated. No one can change the sports teams or the cast members in the school plays. But who's a *Superlative* is really up to the editors. And the bad thing is that the kids who get in that section are usually kids who already have a lot of privilege and already are famous at least in terms of high school. Sometimes you get a good faculty advisor who mixes things up a little, and makes you look at *Superlatives* in a different way, but this year I don't think that's going to happen.

That fame thing—for a lot of us, fame isn't going to be in the cards. I mean going forward when we go out into the world. At least not traditional fame. Or we'll be famous just in our own town for something that a lot of people think is small but maybe isn't. Like making a really good apple pie or being "employee of the month" at an office or being someone who fosters rescue cats or drives old people to the doctor. And probably some people—because of bad luck or bad choices—will be famous for something bad, like becoming a criminal or tragic-bad like dying in a war when they're still young.

I talked to Mom about it because she still has her old high school yearbook, and she showed it to me after we discussed the protest idea. She went to this really teeny high school in Pennsylvania where she grew up. The list of the Superlatives in her yearbook was called *The Best of The Best*—and it listed things like the editors want to keep doing in our yearbook.

Then Mom turned to the pictures of everyone in the senior class and started telling me about different kids.

"This is Hugh," she said. "He helped his dad out in their grocery store. Sometimes he brought in extra food at lunchtime and shared with other kids."

Then she talked about this girl named Mandy who joined the Future Teachers of America and volunteered to read stories to little kids at the library.

"This is George," she said. "He could imitate anyone, like people you would see on TV or in the movies. He always made people laugh, not laugh at other people, just fun laughing."

Mom talked about all these kids, then she said that she wished the nice things she remembered about her classmates were written in the yearbook, so maybe when their kids or grandkids or great-grandkids looked back, they would see those good things. They'd be famous for those things and be remembered for them. Mom said that for most people, their yearbook is the only book that will ever list their name.

So, about the sit-down strike. Martin and I are on the yearbook staff—we're not editors or anything because we're not seniors, but we both joined because we both like to write. Martin's been on the school newspaper, and I got interested in writing in Ms. Marshall's class.

So the editors were talking about the Superlatives, and we said we thought everybody in the whole senior class should be tagged with something nice. Everyone should be famous in their yearbook. When you're a senior, you're eighteen or almost eighteen. You're an adult and ready to start your journey into the real world. Some kids are going to have it tough right off the bat, like Sophie whose mom died of breast cancer last fall. Some kids are going to be doing risky stuff, like Dennis who wants to be a police officer like his dad, and I know a couple kids are going to enlist.

Sure, some kids will do really cool stuff, but some will be like that poem we read in English class about life not being a crystal stair. What I wanted, what Martin and I both wanted and still want, is that the Superlatives section lists one nice thing for all the seniors to be famous for before we start. One story, one nice thing to be tagged with before graduation. Before we start climbing up the stairs.

Thank you for reading this and for not kicking me and Martin off the yearbook. I guess our idea won't happen this year, but we'll be seniors in just a few months and get to be editors ourselves. We've got some really cool plans.

# Skinny Dip

It was cooler here, outside in the dark, sitting on a bench by the bank of the river. Well, it was cooler than it had been at noon, but the night was still hot. The thermometer had dipped into the mid-eighties but then stayed there, stubbornly refusing to budge, even now, hours after sunset. But the sky was clear and showing a thousand stars, the moon was full, and fireflies danced all around them. Mosquitoes, too, but Cherry waved them off as well as she could, determined to prevent them from chasing her away.

"I'm glad for the bench," Gil said. "Somehow, when you hit a certain age, you begin to appreciate the essential importance of a park bench. Back in the day, we'd just sprawl on the grass. Of course, River Bend wasn't even really a park back then. There weren't any benches to sit on even if we wanted to. The town owned the property, but it wasn't developed. The benches and trails, the gazebo and pier, they were all put in about twenty, twenty-five years ago, a few years before you and William moved here. When I was a teen, River Bend was just a good spot for a swim on a hot day or a cuddle on a dark night."

He was quiet a minute, then added, "Val loved it here."

It had only been recently that Gil had started talking about his late wife. Cherry understood. She had lost her husband more than three years ago and recalled the time when she couldn't even talk about him because the saying of his name, simply saying *William*, would undo her.

Now she could talk about him, tell stories, and even laugh as she recalled one of his quips, or an absurd event, or something they had found funny, a happy moment of shared delight.

Cherry's job as manager of the Second Chance Shop, the thrift store that raised money for the Friends of the Hospital, had given her experience in understanding those like Gil, like herself, who had lost partners. And others who had lost parents, or grandparents, or children, or friends. So often, the hospital—the doctors and nurses and social workers—had been kind, and helpful, and gotten them through the unbearable details that came on at the end.

Some of those who grieved would come to Second Chance as a way to say thank you. It was also a way to acknowledge that there would always be those, others, who would need the same kindness and help that they had received. They would drop off donations—sometimes the clothing or belongings of the one that was gone—or write out a check or buy something even if they didn't really need it, or volunteer in the shop.

It wasn't only people with a connection to the hospital who staffed the shop, of course. There were others, like Linus who had a small vineyard and, more importantly, a big heart. And a truck. He did pickups from all the donation bins that were scattered over the county. There was Hannah, a teen who had been sent to them by the school guidance counselor to do mandatory "community service" after some difficulties at school. Hannah had become a happy, everyday presence who talked a mile a minute and made them all laugh. There was Camilla, a grandmotherly sort of person who calmly managed the million details required to make everything work. And so many others who stepped forward to volunteer: Donna, John, Lucy, Sonia, Elias, Hannah's friend Kerry, Camilla's grandson Santiago. So many.

Gil had been one such volunteer. He had arrived after the loss of his wife and offered to lend a hand and found ways to help each and every day. Today he had helped by driving her over to the college after an offer—actually kind of a plea—from the residence hall coordinator to "take whatever you want—*pleeeease*" from the lost, discarded, forgotten, or abandoned items left by last year's crop of college kids. All that stuff had to go before the new crop came in.

Gil, like Linus, had a truck. Said truck was now stuffed with a full load of cardboard cartons. He had asserted, with a grin, that, "Nothing would make me happier than helping you sort and collect college student cast-offs. I can't imagine a better way to spend a sunny Sunday afternoon."

On the way back, they had stopped for supper at a diner Gil knew about where the hamburgers were good, and the tables held jars of daisies along with the usual bottles of ketchup and salt and pepper shakers. It was late when they left. Somehow, they had started talking about Cedar Town history, what it was like in the old days, what it was like when Gil was young. Unlike Cherry, Gil had grown up here, lived here pretty much his whole life except for the time he'd spent in the army. As they came upon River Bend Park, she admitted that, although she had attended concerts at the gazebo, she had never walked the trails or explored the riverbank.

So he'd turned in the drive, parked in the empty lot, and now they were on a bench, under the full moon, looking out at the water, and talking about how they had spent their childhood summers. Cherry had lived in the library, made money by babysitting, and gone to day camp. He'd tinkered with car engines, played baseball, and—when it was hot at night—gone skinny dipping in the river.

"Tell me all about it," Cherry said with a laugh. "I grew up in a city. We swam in a municipal pool. I loved swimming, but it was always in a pool, even at camp. I've never gone skinny dipping in my life."

"*Well,*" he said with a wry smile, "let me see what I can tell you. Hmm. To begin with, someone who's never done it—a novice you might say—might have some misconceptions. Back then, for us, it wasn't the, um, *disrobing* that was the real issue. We boys could shuck off our t-shirts, drop our jeans, and be in the water in nothing flat. No one was going to get more than a two-second flash of … anything."

"And people didn't have cell phones back then," she noted. "Nothing was going to get recorded or shared on social media."

"Exactly. Good thing, too. Might've been a tad embarrassing."

"Don't tell me you were the shy guy at the skinny dip party. I wouldn't believe you. I can't imagine you had anything to be shy about. I mean … I mean …," she realized she was blushing and was thankful for the darkness, "it doesn't seem like you to be shy."

He grinned and shot her a look. "Cherry, did you just imply that I'm, uh, *pretty?*"

She laughed. "I see Hannah has given you her lecture on gender and adjectives. I've heard it enough times so I can paraphrase pretty well: 'Women can be handsome. Men can be pretty. And, anyway, you don't need to focus on appearance, and you don't even need to categorize by women and men. We're all just people. We can just talk about each other and love each other as people.'"

He was nodding in amusement. "Yep. That's Hannah's latest lecture, word for word."

Cherry started to giggle. "I heard her give Camilla the lecture. Camilla listened attentively like she always does, then hugged Hannah, gave her a big kiss on the top of her head, and said, 'You're absolutely right, Hannah-baby. And you're a sweet, pretty, wonderful girl.' Hannah checks and sees Camilla's teasing her, and the two of them crack up and are just rolling."

Gil smiled. They sat quietly for a while. The fireflies still danced. Some had drifted over the river, their light reflecting in the water.

"Skinny dipping as a teen was just easy," Gil said. "Innocent. Natural. Mostly it was just us boys. We'd be out on our bikes or finishing up a ballgame in the field. It'd be August and hot, and we'd swim. We didn't even think about going home to get our suits. And if sometimes the girls jumped in, too, it was still innocent. We thought it was so daring and adult, but what did we know? Not much. Not back then."

"When was the last time you went skinny dipping?"

"Maybe when I was eighteen, maybe twenty."

Cherry thought about what he had said. "You started off saying that with skinny dipping, the disrobing isn't the real issue. So, if not that, what is it then?"

He considered for a minute. Cherry looked at him and thought his expression seemed half amused, half genuinely thoughtful.

"It's not about the throwing off of clothes. It's the throwing off of everything else. You throw off the heat of summer, the chores, the cares. It always seemed to me, that even if you carried the weight of the world on your shoulders, you could throw it off when you dived in the water."

Cherry wrinkled her brow. "I like that way of thinking about it, but maybe there's something else, too. Maybe it's not just about throwing everything off. Maybe it's also about letting something in. I always felt that diving into water was like entering a different world. A world where I got to fly and float and … play."

"And get away from the mosquitoes," he added.

"That, too."

"And get cool on an August night."

"Yes."

They looked at each other, then Cherry stood up and held out her hand. He took it and she pulled him to his feet.

"You said you could get in the water—"

"In nothing flat," he said.

"Bet I can beat you," she said.

"Bet you can't."

"I'll be splashing before your shirt's off."

"Ain't happening."

"Then take the bet."

"What does the winner get?"

"I'll figure that out later," she said, "when I've won."

"Big talk."

"Then prove me wrong."

Gil looked up at the starry sky and laughed. "Okay, you're on."

Cherry's heart was pounding. "Okay, mister. On your mark ... get set—"

They said the last word together.

"*Go!*"

# About the Author

Bette Bono is the author of the historical mystery, time travel novels *The Better Angels* and *Fear Itself* and the short story collections *Neighbors & Other Stories* and *The Second Chance Shop & Other Stories*. Bette has worked as a writer, public school teacher, teachers' union steward, Harvard-trained lawyer, and political analyst. She lives in Connecticut with her family. Learn more at *bettebono.com*.

www.ingramcontent.com/pod-product-compliance
Lightning Source LLC
Chambersburg PA
CBHW051833150726
47998CB00001B/399